About the Book

No one, not even the Governor or Professor Hum-whistel, the famous space detective, knows what is causing the mysterious attack on the western side of Square Toe Mountain. The houses there are breaking up, the statues are falling down, the flowers and vegetables have stopped growing, the veterinarian's office is full of sick animals, and the schools may have to be closed because of a coughing epidemic. What's more, the rainwater tastes like vinegar. Could there be acid in the rain? Where would it come from?

Miss Pickerell resolutely puts the clues together and gets on the trail. In this, her fourteenth adventure, she is joined by her middle nephew, Euphus, and a team of his classmates. They make the mountain search on their bicycles, using pH meters to guide them. Miss Pickerell, following in the Governor's helicopter, defies the danger of the pursuing helicopter that is trying to block her way, and even persuades the President of the United States to take action. There is really no stopping Miss Pickerell!!

Miss Pickerell on the Trail

Miss Pickerell on the Trail

**ELLEN MacGREGOR
and DORA PANTELL
Illustrated by CHARLES GEER**

McGRAW-HILL BOOK COMPANY

NEW YORK · ST. LOUIS · SAN FRANCISCO · AUCKLAND ·
BOGOTÁ · HAMBURG · JOHANNESBURG · LONDON · MADRID ·
MEXICO · MONTREAL · NEW DELHI · PANAMA · PARIS ·
SÃO PAULO · SINGAPORE · SYDNEY · TOKYO · TORONTO

1 2 3 4 5 6 7 8 9 M U M U 8 7 6 5 4 3 2 1

ISBN 0-07-044591-5

LIBRARY OF CONGRESS CATALOGING IN PUBLICATION DATA

MacGregor, Ellen.
Miss Pickerell on the trail.

Summary: Miss Pickerell is joined by her nephew
and a team of his classmates as she tries to discover
what is causing the mysterious attack on the western
side of Square Toe Mountain.
[1. Mystery and detective stories]   I. Pantell,
Dora F.   II. Geer, Charles, ill.   III. Title.
PZ7.M1698Mpd   [Fic]   81-12316
ISBN 0-07-044591-5   AACR2

*For Julius Schwartz,
without whose scientific knowledge
and imagination
the MISS PICKERELL adventures
would barely have been possible.*

Contents

1   MYSTERY ON SQUARE TOE MOUNTAIN   11

2   THE MYSTERY DEEPENS   21

3   MISS PICKERELL FINDS A CLUE   31

4   THE MAYOR INTERRUPTS   41

5   WHO GOES THERE?   50

6   EUPHUS MAKES A DISCOVERY   57

7   ON TO THE CITY COUNCIL   68

8   "WE CAN'T STOP THE RAIN, MISS PICKERELL"   74

9   MAPPING OUT THE BICYCLE PLAN   84

10   THE SEARCH BEGINS   95

11   "EUPHUS TO MISS PICKERELL!   104
     EUPHUS TO MISS PICKERELL!"

12   THE MYSTERIOUS STRANGER   115

13   THE ARRIVAL   122

14   THE CONFRONTATION   130

15   "CALL THE PRESIDENT, MISS PICKERELL"   141

16   THE SOLUTION   149

1

Mystery on Square Toe Mountain

Miss Pickerell set her cup of steaming hot coffee down on Mrs. Broadribb's linoleum-covered kitchen table and stared at the three gentlemen and two ladies sitting there with her. She stared especially hard at Mr. Trilling, Square Toe County's piano tuner and Mrs. Broadribb's best friend.

"I don't believe for one minute," she said to him, as she resolutely pushed her eyeglasses more firmly back on her nose and adjusted a few hairpins that had come loose in her excitement, "I definitely do *not* believe that the frogs in and around our mountain ponds and lakes have suddenly stopped singing."

"Frogs do not *sing*," Mr. Trilling replied icily, while Mrs. Broadribb jutted her chin forward over her ample bosom and vigorously nodded her agreement. "The most frogs can do is croak, or perhaps peep. As an expert in musical sounds, I believe I can safely say that my opinion is correct."

Miss Pickerell felt sorely tempted to tell Mr. Trilling what her seven nieces and nephews thought of his musical abilities. In their unanimous opinion, he made the piano worse every time he came to tune it. But she bit her tongue and turned to Mr. Esticott, Square Toe City's chief train conductor, who was not exactly coughing but was definitely producing a kind of rumble every time he breathed.

"I do hope you're not catching cold, Mr. Esticott," she said. "You seem to be having some trouble when you inhale."

"Also when I exhale, Miss Pickerell," he replied, letting out a deep breath to demonstrate and nearly popping the middle button off his navy-blue uniform jacket as he did so. "In this uncertain weather, everything is possible."

Mr. Rugby, wearing a new tall chef's hat, with the words SQUARE TOE COUNTY DINER, M. RUGBY, PROPRIETOR printed on a red band around it, remarked that his friend, Mr. Kettelson, was also suffering from a congestion in the chest.

"But Mr. Kettelson is not one to leave his hardware store to go see a doctor," he added. "Especially not now when he's doing such a good business with his second-hand wood-burning stoves. The potbelly and the fancy parlor-model types are very popular."

"I don't blame him," Miss Lemon, Square Toe City's assistant head telephone operator, sitting next to Mr. Trilling, added in her high nasal voice. "Doctors these days are *not* what they used to be. Personally, the only medical person I feel confident with is the doctor on daytime television. He *listens* to his patients."

"He's an *actor*, not a doctor," Mr. Trilling snorted. "And he hasn't been doing much listening lately, either. He just keeps carting his patients off to surgery."

"Perhaps you really should see a doctor, Miss Lemon," Mrs. Broadribb suggested. "Your eyes seem to me more pink than usual around the edges."

Miss Lemon blushed. Then she let out a small giggle.

"It's the mascara," she said. "Miss Pickerell's oldest niece, Rosemary, recommended it when I met her in the new five-and-dime store last week. And I thought I might try to wear just a little today. It's my morning off from work."

"Pink mascara!" Mrs. Broadribb exclaimed. "I don't believe there is such a thing. In any case, the color looks more like an irritation to me."

Miss Pickerell nodded her head, while she made a mental note to give her oldest niece a good talking-to about her mascara recommendations. Rosemary, in her opinion, wasn't even old enough to have ideas on the subject.

"Everybody seems to be suffering from something these days," she sighed. "My cow, Nancy Agatha, has been having some eye difficulty lately, too. Her left eye was definitely smarting when I led her out to the pasture this morning. My cat, Pumpkins, noticed it immediately. He kept on licking her face in the hope that this would give her some relief."

"Oh?" Mrs. Broadribb asked.

Miss Pickerell nodded again and reached for the knitting bag and umbrella she had placed on the floor next to her chair.

"Thank you for a lovely breakfast party, Mrs. Broadribb," she said, as she stood up. "I particularly enjoyed the waffles with the thick gooseberry jam on them. But I should be getting back to my farm now. It's almost eleven o'clock and—"

"Oh, no!" Mrs. Broadribb interrupted. "Not until you've heard about what Mr. Trilling and I have discovered."

Miss Pickerell sat down again. She waited patiently.

Mrs. Broadribb exchanged questioning glances with Mr. Trilling. He gestured for her to begin.

"Well," she said finally, "as you know, it's been such a strange spring with so much rain that Mr. Trilling and I haven't gone out much on the long walks we're both so fond of. We took advantage of the fine weather yesterday to go as far as the ponds and the lakes, the ones near Muddington on this side of the mountain. And, of course, I took my bird-watching glasses along."

Again she looked at Mr. Trilling.

"What Mrs. Broadribb is telling you," he continued for her, "is that not only were the frogs silent, but the birds were silent too—"

"Because," Mrs. Broadribb broke in, "because there were no birds there. Not even the robins and starlings and nuthatches that come at this time of year. And the fish . . ."

"The fish," Mr. Trilling said, finishing the sentence for her, "the fish in the lakes and in the river beyond the lakes were dead. All of them!"

"No!" Miss Pickerell gasped. "What *can* be happening?"

"Everything!" Mr. Esticott burst out, after clearing his throat loudly. "Everything is happening these days. Floods, earthquakes, climate changes, oil . . ."

"And mud slides," Mr. Rugby added. "And jets breaking up in midair. And—"

"And oil shortages," Mr. Esticott continued from where he had left off. "Also, robots moving in to take the place of working people. Also—"

"Stop! Stop!" Miss Lemon pleaded, putting her hands over her ears. "Let's talk about something more cheerful, please!"

"Yes, let's," Mrs. Broadribb prompted. "What juicy tidbits do you have for us today, Miss Lemon?"

Miss Lemon blushed again.

"If you mean the things I can't help overhearing when I'm at the switchboard . . ." she began.

Mrs. Broadribb nodded encouragingly.

"There *have* been a number of them," Miss Lemon admitted. "But I'm naming no names, you understand. That wouldn't be right."

"Perhaps just a few little hints here and there?" Mrs. Broadribb pleaded, smiling.

"We wouldn't expect any hints," Miss Pickerell said, giving Mrs. Broadribb a sharp look.

Mrs. Broadribb stopped smiling. Miss Lemon took a deep breath.

"Well, first of all," she whispered, "one of

17

your neighbors on Square Toe Mountain, Miss Pickerell, has had her fortune told. *And* she was advised that she was going to be married soon to a gentleman with a thin black mustache and very large side whiskers."

All eyes turned to Mr. Trilling, who wore a thin black mustache. But he had no whiskers of any kind. Miss Pickerell couldn't help wondering whether it was Mrs. Broadribb who had had her fortune told and whether Mr. Trilling might not one day grow some side whiskers. She decided against it. Miss Lemon would not be so tactless as to repeat Mrs. Broadribb's overheard telephone conversation to her own face in her own house.

"And," Miss Lemon went on, "another neighbor, a gentleman this time, has a wife who is expecting triplets. The doctor is absolutely certain."

"Mr. Sprogg!" Mr. Rugby shouted. "He told everybody. Everybody knows *that*."

"But do you *also* know," Miss Lemon shouted back, "that Mr. Sprogg's house is breaking up? The walls have become pitted and the bricks have turned white. Some of them have crumbled into dust. He called the Governor about it."

"Forevermore!" Miss Pickerell whispered.

"What did the Governor say?" Mrs. Broadribb asked.

"He said he was fully aware of the problem," Miss Lemon replied. "He had already received calls from people in Greensville, Holtsville, and Round View Valley. He had also received an urgent call from our own mayor."

"The Mayor!" Mr. Rugby and Mr. Esticott exclaimed together.

"Yes," Miss Lemon told them. "The Mayor wanted him to know that his two favorite statues on the City Hall lawn, the one of the third United States President sitting and the one of the twenty-sixth United States President standing, were both crumbling."

"And what did the Governor say then?" Mrs. Broadribb asked again.

"He said he had consulted some scientific experts and they said it was probably due to erosion," Miss Lemon stated.

"Erosion?" Mr. Trilling questioned.

"It's the wearing away of the earth's surface by the forces of nature," Miss Pickerell volunteered. "My middle nephew, Euphus, once explained it to me. He was studying about it in school. And I looked it up in my encyclopedia to make sure, in the E volume that you borrowed from me, Mr. Esticott, and still have not returned."

"I told you, Miss Pickerell," Mr. Esticott apologized, "that I'm a slow reader."

"Very slow," Miss Pickerell agreed. "You don't practice enough."

She turned from Mr. Esticott to ask Miss Lemon a question.

"Which force of nature was the Governor referring to when he mentioned erosion?" she wanted to know.

"He didn't," Miss Lemon told her. "He said it was all a mystery to him."

"Mystery, mystery everywhere," Mr. Trilling reflected, singing the words up and down on the scale. "In nature, in music, in poetry, in—"

"Well, this is one mystery that's going to be solved," Miss Pickerell declared, cutting him short and reaching once again for her knitting bag and umbrella. "I'm going right back to my farm and I'm calling the Governor the very minute that I get there. He'll have to make *some* sense out of this . . . this sickness that can infect houses, statues, fish, frogs, people, even my poor Nancy Agatha, all at the same time!!"

2

The Mystery Deepens

From Mrs. Broadribb's back porch Miss Pickerell could look down over two neighboring gardens and across the fields of dandelion and clover to the roof of her own neat barn. And when she squinted her eyes in the direction of the pasture gently sloping up from the barn, she could see that Nancy Agatha was quietly eating her lunch.

"She must be feeling better," Miss Pickerell told herself comfortingly, as she hurried down the steps of the porch and began to walk briskly toward her pasture. "Animals don't eat when they're sick."

But Nancy Agatha, Miss Pickerell observed when she examined her closely, actually seemed to be a little worse. The cow's right eye was somewhat red now, too. As a matter of fact, Miss Pickerell considered thoughtfully, both eyes were beginning to look alarmingly like Miss Lemon's.

"And it *can't* be the mascara," she remarked to Pumpkins, her big black cat, who had interrupted his nap under a maple tree to join her in the pasture. "I'm calling the veterinarian this very minute."

Miss Pickerell did not even bother to take off her hat or put her umbrella and knitting bag away after she unlocked the door to her kitchen. She went straight to the telephone that hung on the wall next to her new yellow refrigerator and dialed Dr. Haggerty's number.

"I've already examined three horses, five dogs, and six cats with the same symptoms," Dr. Haggerty told her almost immediately. "Unfortunately, there's almost nothing I can do to help. How can I when I don't know the cause?"

"Forevermore!" Miss Pickerell breathed when she hung up. "Another mystery! Well, I'm certainly going to call the Governor!"

She proceeded instantly to dial his number.

For his personal use, the Governor had installed a direct-dialing system with a private number that he gave out only to his friends and relations. Miss Pickerell thought that he must have a lot of friends and relations, because the line was practically always busy. It was busy now, too. It was busy for so long that Miss Pickerell felt sure the Governor's wife was on the line.

"And she can go on forever," Miss Pickerell commented to Pumpkins, who was now sitting on top of the refrigerator and watching her. "She's even a longer telephone talker than Rosemary. I'd better call the Mayor. He'll listen because of his statues."

The Mayor did not have direct dialing of any kind. The switchboard operator who answered the telephone listened to Miss Pickerell's reasons for calling and told her she had the wrong number.

"I definitely do *not* have the wrong number," Miss Pickerell replied curtly. "I'm sure the Mayor would be most interested in discussing the erosion problem with me and I have every intention of being put through to him."

"You want to talk to Bridges and Tunnels," the operator's voice said, connecting her with that department before Miss Pickerell could even tell her that she had absolutely no interest in talking to Bridges and Tunnels.

The Bridges and Tunnels voice was more

polite but insisted on transferring her to Highway Control. From Highway Control, Miss Pickerell's call went to Parks and Playgrounds. When she advised Parks and Playgrounds that transferring her around this way was simply a crime, she was put through to Crime Prevention. And when she mentioned to Crime Prevention that she was going to write a letter to the newspapers, she was transferred to Public Relations.

Miss Pickerell's patience was wearing very thin. She said as much to Public Relations.

"This is Miss Pickerell of Square Toe Farm," she shouted the instant the new voice came on the line, "and I am calling to talk to the Mayor. I have already advised your switchboard operator and a number of your city departments that erosion is the basic problem I wish to discuss with him. My middle nephew, Euphus, has told me the meaning of that word, which no one in this office seems to understand. I will now proceed to explain it to you. Erosion is the . . ."

The Mayor's voice came on the line in less than a minute. He sounded as hurried as all the others.

"Good morning, Miss Pickerell," he said, talking very fast. "Or is it good afternoon? I'm never quite sure when I'm so busy work-

24

ing. How is your cow? Nancy Agatha is her name, I believe. Do you remember the time she was lost and my Assistant Sheriff helped you to find her? And how is Pumpkins, the cat? No further problems with either of them, I hope."

The Mayor stopped to take a breath. But he did not pause long enough for Miss Pickerell to be able to say anything. He went right on talking.

"Here at City Hall," he said, "we never cease to have problems. Do you know what the latest one is? A sanitation strike scheduled to start today or tomorrow. Do you know what the streets will look like if we have such a strike, Miss Pickerell? The sidewalks will be lined with garbage. People will get sick, business will suffer, and, personally, I'm starting to feel one of my nervous headaches coming on. Goodbye, Miss Pickerell. Give my love to the animals. And call again. Call any time, Miss Pickerell. Everyone should feel free to talk to the Mayor."

Miss Pickerell's head was swimming. She sighed deeply and dialed the Governor's number again. This time he answered on the first ring. But when she told him about the frogs and the fish and about Miss Lemon's eyes and Nancy Agatha's eyes and what Dr. Haggerty had said and started to tell him about Mr. Sprogg's house, the Governor said that he was aware of many of the problems.

"I have already heard about most of them from the Mayor," he informed her.

"The Mayor's about to have a sanitation strike," Miss Pickerell commented.

"Well, he didn't mention that," the Governor replied. "He was too busy talking about other things."

"About his favorite statues?" Miss Pickerell asked.

"That was yesterday," the Governor said. "Today he talked about the concert hall, which is losing one of its pillars. Ticket holders for this evening's performance are asking for their money back."

"That's only right," Miss Pickerell stated.

"There's no money to give them," the Governor replied. "The concert management has already used it to pay last month's rent. Concert halls seem always to be behind in their rent. But that's the Mayor's problem. I have others."

"Oh?" Miss Pickerell inquired.

"Yes," the Governor replied, sighing. "My wife has just called me about her garden in our Square Toe Mountain cottage. As was announced over the radio, we are staying there while our apartment in the State Capital is being renovated. My poor wife was absolutely shocked when she went into the garden to do some weeding. Her prize flowers, the red rovers she was growing for the flower show, had wilted overnight."

Miss Pickerell could understand her concern.

"And she coughed so much when she spoke to me," the Governor added, "I had to keep asking her to repeat the things she was saying. The conversation took a very long time."

Miss Pickerell understood that part.

"My friend Mr. Esticott, the train conductor, seems to be having some difficulty breathing," she told the Governor. "And I hear from my friend, Mr. Rugby, that Mr. Kettelson, the hardware-store man, is suffering from a chest condition."

"They're not the only ones!," the Governor replied, almost shouting in his excitement. "I've just heard from two movie managers in Plentibush City who have been forced to close their theaters."

"Because of the coughing?" Miss Pickerell asked. "Or because of breathing difficulties?"

"Because of arguments between the coughers and the noncoughers in the audience," the Governor replied. "In one case there was a fist fight and the police had to be called."

"I don't approve of violence," Miss Pickerell told the Governor.

"Of course not," the Governor agreed. "But we are probably going to have more of it. The farmers in Chickering County have called to say they are losing their crops. There will be hunger in our state, Miss Pickerell. There may even be riots."

"We have to get to the bottom of this," Miss Pickerell said firmly.

"How?" the Governor pleaded. "Tell me *how*, Miss Pickerell. I don't even know where to begin."

"Well," Miss Pickerell suggested, "if the scientific experts whom you consulted said that the problem was erosion, which, my middle nephew says, is the wearing away of the earth's surface, it seems to me that..."

The Governor's bitter laugh rang out over the telephone.

"Erosion!" he repeated. "If the cause is erosion, *where* is this erosion coming *from*, Miss Pickerell? And what does the wearing away of the earth's surface have to do with my wife's cough and your cow's eyes and Mr. Kettelson's chest condition? Your scientist friend, Professor Humwhistle, has told me he believes that everything is connected, Miss

Pickerell. But even he doesn't know the *exact cause* at the moment."

"We have to find out," Miss Pickerell told him. "We dare not give up."

"Who said anything about giving up?" the Governor asked instantly. "I have always worked hard to keep this state on the map. I will *not* be forced to declare it a disaster area. I will *not* let totally unexplained events bring me to my knees. But the mystery definitely deepens, Miss Pickerell. And I'm at my wit's end, I tell you, absolutely at my wit's end."

3

Miss Pickerell Finds a Clue

"I have to think," Miss Pickerell told herself, when she put the telephone back in its cradle and started taking the long black pins out of her hat. "I have to *think*."

But no matter how hard she tried, no clues to solve the mystery came into her mind. She even began walking up and down her kitchen floor because that sometimes helped her to think. It didn't this time, though.

"Well, I'll just have to stop forcing myself," she said, talking out loud. "I'll have to think about something else. And maybe the idea will suddenly pop into my head."

She looked around the kitchen, wondering what she might do to occupy her mind while she waited for the idea. There didn't seem to be anything she needed to do. She had polished her big brass tea kettle yesterday. And she had rearranged her rocks from Mars, and the moon, and the weather station in outer space the day before yesterday. All clearly labeled, they stood in a row on the shelf above the windowsill. Miss Pickerell nearly shivered when she remembered those perilous adventures.

"Never again!" she told herself, as she walked past her sink and then past the broom closet that stood opposite her window. "Never again will I get off my nice peaceful farm to—"

She turned suddenly to take another look at her broom closet. That certainly needed a good cleaning up, she knew.

"And I should have attended to it a long time ago," she told herself.

She opened the closet door and stared up at the piles of stiff paintbrushes and bottles of dried-up furniture varnishes jammed between the brooms and the pails and the mops. The job was going to take all day.

"Not if I throw most of the things out," she told herself firmly. "It's plain silly to keep them when I'll never use them again."

But she wasn't able to work as quickly as she had hoped. One by one, she carefully examined every item before she finally decided to get rid of it. She had just finished heaping up a pile of worn-out cleaning cloths and half-empty jars of old wallpaper glue when Euphus, her middle nephew, appeared at the kitchen door.

"I need to look something up in your encyclopedia," he said breathlessly. "It's for my environment-ecology class. Excuse me. I'm in a hurry."

He raced into the small hallway next to the kitchen, where Miss Pickerell kept her set of encyclopedias. Then, just as fast, he returned with the W volume and sat down to examine it at the kitchen table.

"It's about the chemical properties of water," he explained to Miss Pickerell. "We're testing water's properties during our school spring vacation. We want to have everything all ready before we go back next week."

"Just whom are you referring to when you say *we*?" Miss Pickerell asked.

"Oh, some of my pals," Euphus replied. "I'm in charge of the experiment because I'm the smartest in science."

Miss Pickerell felt very proud of her middle nephew. He was extremely good in science. But she didn't think he should be the one to say so. She made a mental note to talk to him about this when she had more time. At the moment she was too busy making up her mind about whether or not she should throw out the cord that belonged to a broken electric iron. The cord could come in handy someday. Still, it hadn't for over a year and . . .

"We're gathering samples of water and testing them for acidity with our pH meters," Euphus went on to tell her.

Miss Pickerell had no idea what a pH meter was. And she couldn't care less. She certainly had no intention of getting into a discussion of pH meters now.

"Have you found what you were looking for in the encyclopedia?" she asked.

"I was just checking," Euphus told her. "It's exactly the way I thought it was."

He got up to turn on the small radio that stood on top of the refrigerator. The Governor's voice boomed out.

"It's entirely possible," he was saying, "that the chest conditions may turn out to be an epidemic. In that case, we will not be opening the schools after the spring vacation. I will keep the public informed."

Miss Pickerell gasped. She turned the radio off.

"I'd like that," Euphus remarked. "It would give us more time for our other project. That one's about frogs' eggs. We're studying about animals, too, in our class. About animals and water and soil and air. Anyway, we went up to Muddington this morning to look for frogs' eggs. We couldn't find any."

Miss Pickerell was not surprised. How could there be any frogs' eggs when there were no frogs? Mr. Trilling had definitely said that he didn't hear any frogs when he and Mrs. Broadribb went on their walk along the ponds and lakes in Muddington.

"Then," Euphus continued, "we went over to the other side, the eastern side of the mountain, and we found lots. We have all the eggs we need now."

Dried-up paintbrush in one hand and a strip of worn-out masking tape in the other, Miss Pickerell stood stock still. She stared at Euphus.

"What did you say?" she asked. "Tell me again what you said, Euphus. Tell me in *exactly* the same words."

"We went to the other side, the eastern side of the mountain, and we found lots," Euphus repeated absently. "We have—"

"Never mind the rest," Miss Pickerell told him. "Please sit down, Euphus, and draw me

a map. A map that shows all the cities and villages on the western side of the mountain."

"That's easy," Euphus said.

He turned the pages of the encyclopedia, found a blank space, and was about to draw the outlines of the mountainside with his ball-point pen when Miss Pickerell snatched the book away from him. She quickly handed him a pad of yellow paper that she took out of a cabinet drawer. Euphus tore off the first sheet, which had Miss Pickerell's laundry list on it. On the second sheet he made an outline of the west side of the mountain and placed a number of circles inside. He printed the names of the places neatly above each circle.

"This is Greenville," he said, as he put the name down. "And this is Holtsville and Round View Valley and Muddington and Wicklaw and Plentibush City and Square Toe County and . . ."

"That's enough," Miss Pickerell told him.

"I can do more," Euphus offered.

Miss Pickerell shook her head.

"Greenville, Holtsville, and Roundview Valley are the places Miss Lemon mentioned when she said the Governor received telephone complaints," she murmured, as she began pacing the floor again. "And Muddington is the place where Mr. Trilling heard no frogs. And Wicklaw is where Mr. Sprogg lives. And Plentibush City is where they closed the movie houses. And Chickering County is where the farmers are losing their crops. And Square Toe County is where so many people and animals are sick. *And* they are *all* on this *western* side of the mountain. *Something* is *definitely connected*, the way Professor Humwhistel said it was."

Euphus gave her a very puzzled look.

"I believe," Miss Pickerell said softly, "I believe I have found a clue."

"A clue to what?" Euphus asked.

"To a series of mysteries I don't have time to explain," Miss Pickerell announced. "At least, not for the time being."

Euphus shrugged his shoulders.

"They're probably not important," he said. "I have to go now. Call me if you want any more maps, Aunt Lavinia."

"Thank you, Euphus," Miss Pickerell replied. "I don't believe I will need any more."

She put on her hat again and, thinking that the weather might turn colder, she took her long, gray, button-down sweater out of the hall closet. Then she carefully folded Euphus's map into her knitting bag and picked up her umbrella.

"I'm going to see Professor Humwhistel," she said to Pumpkins, who was following her out of the kitchen door. "If anyone can figure out the meaning of what I have discovered, it is a detective. And if anyone has had a lot of experience tracking down strange clues, it is Professor Humwhistel, who is a space detective. Yes, Pumpkins, you are coming with me. You and Nancy Agatha, too. We're all going to see Professor Humwhistel together."

4

The Mayor Interrupts

Miss Pickerell always took her animals with her when she went out in her automobile. Nancy Agatha stood in the trailer that Miss Pickerell could attach to the back of the car. The trailer had a red-fringed awning over it to protect the cow from the rain or from too much sun. Pumpkins sometimes sat in the trailer with Nancy Agatha. Most of the time he settled himself in the front seat next to Miss Pickerell, or on her lap.

The cow's eyes were tearing, Miss Pickerell observed, when she led her into the trailer. Nancy Agatha seemed to be happy about the ride, though. Miss Pickerell thought this was encouraging. She said so while she was wiping the tears away with a piece of soft tissue and gently patting the cow's head.

"We're going to visit Professor Humwhistel," she told her. "He'll know what to do. You'll see."

The ride down the mountain was not a pleasant one. A thick yellow fog lay over everything on the private lane leading down from the farm to the highway. The trees and hedges, which should have looked bright and green with the coming of spring, were limp and woefully bedraggled. Miss Pickerell could hardly bear to look at them.

"More mysterious symptoms!" she muttered, as she turned her eyes away and raised

her speed to her maximum of thirty-five miles per hour.

On the crowded highway leading to Square Toe City and Professor Humwhistel's office, Miss Pickerell drove in the right-hand lane to get out of the way of the honking and shouting from the cars behind her. And she kept calling back to Nancy Agatha in the trailer to make her feel better.

"We're almost there," she told her, as they passed the public library, which badly needed a new coat of paint, and the Square Toe General Store, where Miss Pickerell shopped for wool in the Why Not Knit It Department.

When she parked the automobile in front of the tall brick building where Professor Humwhistel worked, she asked Pumpkins to keep Nancy Agatha company in the trailer. She also told them both that she would not be gone long.

The girl at the lobby reception desk, who had once worked in the Why Not Knit It Department, smiled broadly when she saw Miss Pickerell. Miss Pickerell smiled back.

"I suppose you want to see Professor Humwhistel," the receptionist said. "To congratulate him on his promotion."

"Oh?" Miss Pickerell asked.

"Oh, yes," the girl went on. "He was promoted to First Assistant Chief yesterday. He is now in complete charge of tracking down meteors, receiving messages from outer space, and even looking into all reports about flying saucers in this neighborhood. He has a brand-new office, too. Room 2203 in the tower. You can take one of the express elevators on the right."

Miss Pickerell hated express elevators. They made her dizzy. But she thrust this problem out of her mind. She walked quickly into an open express elevator, pressed the button, and kept her eyes shut until the door opened itself up again on the twenty-second floor.

Professor Humwhistel's new office, she could see from his open doorway, was very different from the one he had been in before. The walls were painted a deep blue, the charts that hung on them were all framed in bright red, and two rows of blinding lights ran along wooden bars from one end of the ceiling to the other. There wasn't a window in sight. Miss Pickerell did not approve. What was the point of having an office in a tower, she asked herself, if one couldn't enjoy the view?

But Professor Humwhistel had not

changed. He still wore his old-fashioned vest buttoned up to his chin and his big gold watch still dangled from his vest pocket. And, as always, he was searching for matches with which to light his pipe. He was just leaning over in his red-leather swivel chair to reach for some matches at the far end of his desk when he realized he had a visitor.

"Why, Miss Pickerell!" he exclaimed, getting up immediately and walking over to greet her. "How very nice to see you!"

Miss Pickerell came directly to the point.

"Professor," she said, "I congratulate you on your promotion. But I have come here about an entirely different matter. I wish to consult you as a detective."

Professor Humwhistel swallowed twice. He also stopped to clean his gold-rimmed eyeglasses with a big white handkerchief.

"A . . . a crime detective?" he spluttered. "That . . . that is not exactly my line, Miss Pickerell. I wouldn't be of much help to you, I'm afraid. I couldn't . . ."

"You can be a very great help," Miss Pickerell interrupted. "I have come with a clue to the recent mysterious happenings. Personally, I think they are all related."

"Ah . . . ah, yes," the professor replied. "The recent mysterious happenings. I have heard something about them from the Governor."

He pulled a chair up to the side of his desk for Miss Pickerell. Then he sat down in his own chair behind the desk and looked inquiringly at her.

"If the Governor has not supplied you with a full-enough description of the problems, I can do so," Miss Pickerell volunteered.

"I don't believe that will be necessary," the professor replied, while he puffed on his half-lit pipe.

"In that case," Miss Pickerell went on, "I will simply present you with the map that Euphus has drawn. It shows *all* the trouble places. *And* they are *all* on the west side of Square Toe Mountain."

She spread the map out on the desk. Professor Humwhistel peered over his glasses to inspect Euphus's printing more closely. Every once in a while he raised his eyes to look admiringly at Miss Pickerell.

"Yes," he said finally. "You have done it, Miss Pickerell. You have given us our first clue. I think we can definitely state now that something is attacking the west side of Square Toe Mountain."

"*Attacking* the west side of Square Toe Mountain!" Miss Pickerell repeated almost mechanically. *"Attacking* the ... *Who?* *What* ...?"

Professor Humwhistel did not answer immediately. He took some fresh tobacco out of his pocket and began to refill his pipe. He sat looking at it thoughtfully.

"You were saying, Professor ..." Miss Pickerell prompted him.

"Yes," the professor replied. "I was about to say that ..."

The telephone rang before the professor could finish his sentence. The Mayor was calling. His voice was so loud that Miss Pickerell could hear every word he said.

"The sanitation strike has started," he told Professor Humwhistel. "The workers have still another grievance now. They refuse to pick up the bricks and rocks that are crumbling all over the city. You must come and tell them that the garbage will give us all typhoid or typhus or the bubonic plague or whatever those diseases were that people used to get from unsanitary conditions. You're a scientist and they'll listen to *you.* And there must be some new scientific way of disposing of the garbage, too. Professor, I insist ..."

"Yes, yes," Professor Humwhistel said. "Immediately!"

Miss Pickerell ran with him toward the elevator.

"You were about to say . . ." she reminded him.

"I was about to say," the professor continued, as the elevator they entered whizzed down to the lobby, "that I can only hazard a guess, at this time, as to who or what the attacker is."

The elevator door slid open. Professor Humwhistel rushed to the staff parking lot in back of the building.

"And," he added to Miss Pickerell, who

was rushing with him, "I have no idea at all where the attack is coming from."

"Forevermore!" Miss Pickerell whispered.

She stood watching the professor roar off on his green-and-orange motorcycle. She was growing more and more furious by the minute. She felt absolutely certain that the professor would have talked to her about his guess, *if* the Mayor hadn't interrupted.

"Well," she told herself, as she walked around the building to her waiting automobile and trailer, "well, I'm certainly going to think twice before I vote for *that man* again."

5

Who Goes There?

The instant Miss Pickerell got into her automobile, she knew that something was wrong with Pumpkins. He had moved from the trailer into the front seat, where he lay looking listless and unhappy. When Miss Pickerell spoke to him, he picked his head up for a moment. Then he lay back again. He also coughed twice and sneezed five times in a row.

"We're going to see Dr. Haggerty!" Miss Pickerell stated immediately. "We're going right now. There must be something he can do."

Dr. Haggerty's office and outside yard, at the edge of Square Toe City, were both very crowded when Miss Pickerell got there. Mrs. Pickett, Miss Pickerell's nearest neighbor, was sitting in the waiting room with the pet lamb that Miss Pickerell had once given her. Mr. Kettelson was also waiting. He was holding the brown-and-white dog he had adopted to keep him company in the store when business was slow. The housekeeper from the Home for Retired and Disabled Animals was standing outside. Dr. Haggerty had already treated Homer, the deaf old plow horse, who lived at the Home.

"That horse understands more than most humans," the housekeeper commented to Miss Pickerell. "You should have seen how grateful he was when Dr. Haggerty put some salve around his eyes to soothe them."

Miss Pickerell nodded approvingly. She was a great believer in salves.

But Dr. Haggerty warned her, when he provided some for Nancy Agatha, that the salve would treat only the symptoms. The same was true of the tablets and cough mixture he was giving her for Pumpkins.

"I have already given both animals the first dose of their medicines," he went on to explain. "You are to repeat it every four hours until the animals go to sleep. Start all over again in the morning."

"Oh, I will! I will!" Miss Pickerell replied eagerly.

Dr. Haggerty sighed.

"I don't really know whether the medicines will help," he added hesitantly. "Unfortunately, I can do no more until I know the cause."

"I understand," Miss Pickerell said, choking back the sobs she felt rising up in her throat.

"Mr. Kettelson and Mrs. Pickett feel very

upset too," Dr. Haggerty said sympa-
thetically.

"I know," Miss Pickerell said.

Her heart was breaking for all the poor
sick animals. And there was nothing she
could do to help any of them. She climbed
wearily back into her automobile.

The ride up to the farm was even more de-

pressing than it had been coming down. The fog had grown still thicker. Scattered rain began to fall when Miss Pickerell made the turn onto her private road. By the time she approached the hydrangea bushes that marked the halfway distance up the road, the rain had become a downpour.

"Oh dear!" Miss Pickerell exclaimed.

The words came out as a distinct wheeze. Miss Pickerell stopped driving for an instant to repeat the words and to listen to herself carefully.

"I'm beginning to sound like Mr. Esticott," she whispered, as she drove on. "And he was right. It's just as hard to exhale as it is to inhale."

She made straight for the barn when she reached the top of the hill. She milked Nancy Agatha and told her she was looking much better.

Then, because she didn't think Pumpkins should walk back in the rain, she unhitched the trailer and drove the automobile up to the gate outside her kitchen garden. She carried him under her sweater as she ran across the garden and up the stairs.

At the top of the stairs Miss Pickerell stood absolutely still and stared. She couldn't believe what she saw. The house was all lit up. *Someone* was inside.

A thousand terrible thoughts raced through her mind. The worst were about secret agents who would stop at nothing. In one movie she had seen, the villainous agent had nearly poisoned the heroine by persuading her to drink innocent-looking tea that had poison in it.

"That's enough!" Miss Pickerell told herself, as she tried to get a hold on these wild ideas she was imagining. "I'm being plain ridiculous. And I *don't* think it's thieves in there, either. Thieves would *not* leave all the lights on. And certainly not in the middle of the afternoon when it would attract attention to them. Well, I'm going to find out for myself!"

She took a hesitant step toward the door and rapped on it.

"Who . . . who . . .?" she called.

Her voice came out as a hoarse whisper. No one answered. The only sound was Pumpkins's loud meow, as he struggled out from under her sweater and leaped to the ground.

She rapped again, with her unfurled umbrella this time.

Footsteps sounded on the other side. They came closer and closer.

"Who goes there?" Miss Pickerell screamed, as she made an enormous effort not to remember any more old movies, told herself firmly that she would, of course, not be offered even a sip of poisoned tea, and waited for the door to open.

6

Euphus Makes a Discovery

It was her oldest niece, Rosemary, who stood on the other side of the door. She was wearing Miss Pickerell's winter bathrobe, and a towel was wrapped around her hair. Miss Pickerell observed instantly that it was her very best guest towel. She also saw that a mixture of dirty water and loose mud was oozing out of Rosemary's open-toe sandals and that her niece was shivering under the heavy flannel robe.

"What—? What—?" Miss Pickerell gasped.

Rosemary did not answer. She turned and led the way out of the kitchen, through the little hallway next to the kitchen, past the extra pantry that Miss Pickerell had installed on the other side of the hallway, and up to the parlor in the front of the house.

From inside the parlor came both the

booming voice of a television announcer describing the latest horrors of the mystery, and the distinct sound of splashing water. Two boys, coughing and sneezing at the same time, were placing jars with water dripping out of them on the polished coffee table in front of the sofa. Euphus, also sneezing, sat in the middle of the sofa, directing three other boys to transfer still more jars from the floor. He was so absorbed in what he was doing that he didn't even notice Rosemary or Miss Pickerell.

"Euphus!" Miss Pickerell shouted, staring at the moist hair and water-soaked shoes of her middle nephew and his friends. "Turn off that television set and the lights. And get out of those wet shoes and socks. All of you! That goes for you too, Rosemary. I'm making you something hot to drink this instant. Before you all catch your death of cold—"

"Oh, no!" Euphus pleaded, "We're just starting on our experiment and—"

"Into the kitchen, with dry feet and hair!" Miss Pickerell ordered. "And you can bring all those jars into the kitchen, too. They don't belong in my parlor."

She hurried to boil two large kettles of water and to prepare steaming hot mugs of her favorite peppermintade. She put plenty of tea and honey in with the peppermint. Because she also believed in food to help prevent a cold, she prepared heaping plates of peanut-butter sandwiches as well.

"Now then!" she said, when Euphus and Rosemary and the others were settled around the kitchen table and she sat with Pumpkins on her lap. "Now then, what is this all about?"

Euphus took a deep breath.

"It's simple," he said. "My team and I went up on the mountain to collect water samples for the project I told you about. Rosemary just tagged along."

"I didn't!" Rosemary shouted. "You said you needed me to help with the—"

"I didn't want to hurt your feelings," Euphus replied.

"When did you ever stop to—?" Rosemary screamed.

Miss Pickerell waved the argument aside.

"Go on with your explanation, Euphus," she said.

"Well," Euphus continued, "we got caught in the rain and we ran down here for shelter. You weren't home, but I knew where you kept your extra key. So I got it from under the mat and we came in. That's all. Can we go back to working on the testing now, please, Aunt Lavinia?"

Miss Pickerell looked out of the window. It was still raining too hard for her to send the children home. The water tests would at least keep them busy while she attended to her own business. She *had* to get back to that broom closet.

"Very well," she agreed. "*Provided* you don't spill any water on the floor. *And* provided you don't chatter!"

"Oh, no," Euphus promised. "We won't say a word. But, look! Look at these jars, Aunt Lavinia! The ones that we lined up on the cabinet have water in them from the ponds on the east side of the mountain. The ones on the counter top have the pond water from the west side. And the ones we still haven't brought in from the parlor have rainwater in them. My team is going to bring them in now."

Miss Pickerell gave up. Euphus and his friends talked on and on. Every once in a while, Euphus also insisted that she come and watch what they were doing.

"See?" he asked, as he and his teammates inserted their pH meters into the first row of jars. "We're measuring the water properties now. That's what pH meters do. They measure the acidity and alkalinity in soil, water, and other fluids."

The pond water in the first jars measured pH 8.

"That means it's very low in acidity," Euphus explained. "The pH scale runs from pH zero for very acid to pH 14 for very alkaline. On the scale, pH 7 is neutral, neither acid nor alkaline. Rosemary is going to write down the figures for us."

"I will *not*," Rosemary said.

But she changed her mind when Euphus admitted that she would be able to figure out the pH averages much faster than he could. She picked up the pad that had had the laundry list on it and made three columns, heading the first one EAST, the second one WEST, and the third one RAIN. She recorded the pH measurements for each of the east jars in the first column and announced that they averaged about pH 8, slightly alkaline. Euphus and his friends went on to measure the second row of jars.

"Wow!" Euphus shouted, as he and his team carefully scrutinized the measurements, which Rosemary had recorded as averaging about pH 5. "They're different for the west jars. Very different! Did you hear what I said, Aunt Lavinia?"

"I heard," Miss Pickerell said, looking out from the broom closet where she was reorganizing the cleaning supplies she had definitely decided not to throw away. "How are they different?"

"The acidity is higher," Euphus told her. "Much, *much* higher!"

The acidity in the jars filled with rainwater was still higher. It averaged pH 2 in Rosemary's column.

"That's almost at the bottom of the scale!" Euphus exclaimed. "You see, every unit drop represents a *ten-fold increase* in acidity."

"Oh?" Miss Pickerell asked politely.

"The pH of the rainwater is a thousand times as acid as the west pond water! And a million times as acid as the east pond water!" Euphus burst out. "And my science teacher said rainwater was pure. Wait till I tell him about the discovery I made. He'll have the surprise of his life. He'll—"

He interrupted himself to sneeze again.

"I'm not catching cold," he said to Miss Pickerell quickly. "Really, I'm not, Aunt Lavinia. The acid in the rainwater is what's making me sneeze. It's sour. And it tastes just like vinegar."

"You didn't drink it?" Miss Pickerell asked, horrified.

"Not out of the jars, we didn't," Euphus answered. "But we tasted it when the rain fell into our mouths. It got into our eyes too and it made them—"

Miss Pickerell decisively shut the door of her broom closet. An idea had come into her head. A perfectly clear, sensible idea! She couldn't actually imagine why she hadn't thought of it before. She couldn't even i- magine why Professor Humwhistel hadn't thought of it. But maybe that was one of the things he was *guessing*. Well, *she* was *not* guess- ing *now*!

"Euphus!" she exclaimed, as she walked briskly into the middle of the room. "Profes- sor Humwhistel told me today that some- thing was attacking the west side of the mountain."

Rosemary stopped writing in her columns. Euphus and his friends stopped talking.

"He also told the Governor," Miss Pick- erell went on, "that everything was con- nected—the crumbling of Mr. Sprogg's house and the condition of the crops and of Mr.

Kettelson's chest and lots more. I don't know *just* how or why they are connected *yet*, but I agree completely with the professor. What's more, I believe the attack is coming down from the sky."

"From the *sky*?" Rosemary, Euphus, and his friends repeated.

"Yes," Miss Pickerell replied. "It's the acid in the rainwater that made you sneeze, Euphus. And it is the acid in the rain that is spoiling the red ramblers the Governor's wife is growing, and ruining the crops that the farmers . . ."

"Make a note at the bottom of the page!" Euphus shouted to Rosemary. "Please write down, 'ACID RAIN IS ATTACKING US.' "

"I was about to add," Miss Pickerell went on, "that since the rain is carried by the winds—"

"The westerly winds," Euphus interrupted.

"Of course, the westerly winds," Miss Pickerell replied. "The rain clouds come in from the west."

"Make another note—" Euphus began.

"Never mind the notes, Euphus," Miss Pickerell told him. "You have the *evidence* of the acidity content in your jars. I am taking them and the record of your measurements to

Professor Humwhistel. I am *not* going to let the people and the animals and everything else that I love become disaster victims. I am getting on the trail to track this attacker down!"

"Bravo!" Euphus's team shouted together.

"Right on!" Euphus added, applauding.

Pumpkins, who was eating from his dish near the refrigerator, jumped up on the table to see what the excitement was all about.

7

On to the City Council

The woman who picked up Professor Humwhistel's telephone said that he had not yet returned to his office. She had no idea where he might be. She was only his part-time secretary, she explained, and she didn't keep track of his comings and goings.

"I know where he is," Miss Lemon's unmistakable voice broke in.

"Why, Miss Lemon!" Miss Pickerell exclaimed. "I thought this was your day off."

"I'm working the evening shift on overtime," Miss Lemon told her. "It starts at five o'clock. I'm a half-hour early, but I wanted to be sure to get here on time."

"Of course," Miss Pickerell agreed. "That's always a good policy."

"The telephone supervisor called to ask me

if I would please help out on the evening shift," Miss Lemon went on. "She said she wanted to be sure the switchboard was completely covered because of the emergency meeting."

"What emergency meeting?" Miss Pickerell asked instantly.

"You mean that you haven't heard?" Miss Lemon asked. "I thought everybody knew. The City Council is having an emergency meeting. That's where Professor Humwhistel is right now. The Mayor's there, too. And the Governor. And representatives from the public at large, including Mr. Sprogg, whose house is still crumbling. They're talking about garbage disposal."

"Oh?" Miss Pickerell inquired.

"You see," Miss Lemon continued, "Professor Humwhistel was not able to persuade the sanitation workers to stop striking. And he didn't have any new practical ideas for getting rid of the garbage. Oh, please excuse me, Miss Pickerell! There's another call coming in. But I did manage to tell you where the professor is, in case you want to find him."

"Yes, thank you very much, Miss Lemon," Miss Pickerell replied, thinking that there were occasions when Miss Lemon's eavesdropping at the switchboard came in very handy.

Actually, she no longer needed to find Professor Humwhistel. She had a better idea. She was going to present the evidence to the City Council. She was going to give *them* a good piece of her mind and see to it that they got on the trail *with* her. And she was going to get started immediately.

"All jars are to be covered," she said to Euphus and his team, the minute she got off the telephone. "Be sure the covers are on tight. And Rosemary, please get some clean labels from the desk upstairs and put them on the jars. Euphus will tell you which jars to label EAST, WEST, and RAIN. I am taking the pH measurements and the water samples to the City Council. I am showing them to the Mayor."

"I have more," Euphus offered, pointing to two jars that stood in the corner behind Miss Pickerell's stepladder. "More water samples, I mean. We took some from the rain puddles in the City Hall Plaza yesterday. The Mayor will like those. And he can taste the water too, if he wants."

"I doubt that tasting will be necessary," Miss Pickerell replied. "But the Mayor can have some of his City Hall water, if he wishes."

Her wheezing was getting worse. She tried to clear her throat. It didn't help. She decided to ignore the matter. She picked up her knitting bag and umbrella from the telephone stool where she had left them and made sure that her hat was on straight.

"You're not going to the City Council in *that* old hat?" Rosemary, who was watching her, exclaimed.

"I'm not going to a fashion show," Miss Pickerell told her.

"And that sweater!" Rosemary protested. "You can at least change your sweater."

Miss Pickerell looked out of the window. It had stopped raining. But the sky was still full of clouds and the wind seemed to have grown stronger. She took off the gray sweater and changed into her heavier brown one.

The jars and labels were all ready. Euphus and his team had put their shoes and socks back on. Rosemary said she was going to get dressed, too.

"I can't wait till I get home to blow-dry my hair," she said.

"I'll drive you home," Miss Pickerell told her. "It's on my way. Then Euphus and I will go on to the City Council meeting."

Euphus jumped out of his chair.

"You mean I can go with you?" he asked. "To explain . . . ?"

"As clearly and as *briefly* as possible," Miss Pickerell warned him.

She turned to say goodbye to Euphus's friends and to thank them for the good work they had done. They offered to help carry the jars on their way out. Miss Pickerell showed them where her shopping cart was and suggested they stack the jars there.

"Then you can carry the cart down the stairs and wheel it across the garden to the gate," she told them. "I am driving the automobile back to the barn to get the trailer and my cow."

Pumpkins meowed his intention of going along as soon as Miss Pickerell walked toward the door. She asked Rosemary to hold him for her until she got back from the barn.

When Miss Pickerell returned with Nancy Agatha in the trailer, she walked back to the house to lock her kitchen door. She also asked Euphus to take the extra key out from under the mat and to place it behind the geranium pot that stood on the outside windowsill. And she made sure that Euphus had remembered to take the pad of paper with the pH measurements along. Then, with him on one side of her and Rosemary holding Pumpkins in her arms on the other, she marched down the steps and across her kitchen garden.

8

"We Can't Stop the Rain, Miss Pickerell"

Nancy Agatha was mooing contentedly in the trailer, but Miss Pickerell knew this was only because the cow felt glad to have company. She did not look much better. Pumpkins went to sleep on Miss Pickerell's lap as soon as she settled herself behind the steering wheel. Miss Pickerell did not believe this was a good sign, either. Pumpkins was usually too curious even to think of going to sleep when he rode in the automobile.

Miss Pickerell drove with extra care on the way down the mountain. She did not want to jostle the jars lined up in the shopping cart. Euphus and Rosemary, sitting in the back with the cart between them, were watching it. But Miss Pickerell liked to be absolutely certain. After Rosemary got out, Miss Pickerell cautioned Euphus to hold onto the cart with both hands. She and Euphus carried the cart out of the automobile carefully when they arrived at the City Hall. Euphus waited at the door while Miss Pickerell looked for a place to park. She was able to squeeze into a space behind the Governor's official car.

The City Council room on the main floor was very crowded. Miss Pickerell could not even find a place to sit down. And when she told Mr. Trilling, who was acting as sergeant at arms, that she wanted to speak, he said it was impossible.

"You're not on the agenda, Miss Pickerell," he informed her. "You should have told us a long time ago that you intended to speak."

"I didn't know about the meeting a long time ago," Miss Pickerell retorted icily. "And I have as much right as anybody else here to have my say."

Mrs. Broadribb, standing next to Mr. Trilling and looking very superior, gestured for him to give her a number. Mr. Trilling took a slip of paper with a number on it out of an old candy box he was carrying.

"You can have a number, Miss Pickerell," he stated. "But it's useless. There are twenty-five numbers ahead of yours. You'll never be reached."

Mrs. Broadribb said that she agreed.

"After all," she added, "this meeting can't go on all night. Most of us haven't even had our dinners."

Miss Pickerell, with Euphus close behind, wheeled the cart to the side of the room. She refused two seats that gentlemen in a back row offered her, moved on to a spot nearer the front, and looked around. The Governor, the Mayor, Professor Humwhistel, and all the members of the City Council were seated at a long table up front. The Mayor was in his shirt sleeves and wore no tie. The Governor had on a light tan suit that exactly matched the gloves and the walking stick he had placed on the table.

The meeting was already in progress. Mr. Sprogg had the floor. He was arguing against a recommendation for garbage disposal made by the local librarian.

"What does a librarian know about garbage disposal?" he was asking. "She may know about books, I grant you. But even my wife, who is certainly not an expert, even my three unborn children would say that her method is not practical. It takes a working man to understand such things and I propose that—"

"I'm a working man," the owner of the gas

station at the foot of Miss Pickerell's private road called out. "Nobody has asked for my recommendation. Nobody has—"

"I see nothing impractical about my suggestion," the librarian shouted, interrupting. "And I don't see that Mr. Sprogg's unborn children have anything to do with it. What's more, I'm a working person, too. I work very hard in the library. I make a motion that Mr. Sprogg's remarks that refer to me as impractical should be taken out of the minutes of this meeting."

A number of people clapped their hands and shouted, "Hooray!" Mr. Sprogg booed. The Mayor banged on the table with his gavel. No one paid the least bit of attention to him until he pointed to the door. Everyone turned to see what he was pointing at. Pumpkins, meowing at the top of his lungs, was walking in.

"Oh!" Miss Pickerell shrieked. "It's . . . it's . . ."

Pumpkins made several leaps when he heard her, the last one right to the top of the shopping cart. Miss Pickerell quickly lifted him out.

"I'm . . . I'm sorry," she apologized. "I must have forgotten to close the windows in my automobile. I was so excited about these water samples that my middle nephew, Euphus, has collected. I brought all the jars so that I could present them as evidence."

"Evidence?" the Mayor, banging again, screamed. "Evidence of *what*, Miss Pickerell?"

"But you know all about the mystery, Mr. Mayor," Miss Pickerell said, looking at him in surprise. "You, yourself, called the Governor to tell him about the statues on your lawn, the ones of the third and of the twenty-sixth President that are crumbling away. And about the concert hall that was losing one of its pillars."

The Mayor and the Governor glanced at each other.

"And the Governor knows about the crops that are failing," Miss Pickerell went on, "and that we may all go hungry and have riots in the streets."

The Governor nodded to the Council members.

"And I haven't even mentioned the frogs and the birds and the fish that are dying and the strange sicknesses that so many people and animals are suffering from," Miss Pickerell added. "And—"

"Am I to understand that you know the cause of all this?" the Mayor interrupted.

Miss Pickerell, trying to collect her

thoughts and to keep Pumpkins quiet at the same time, nodded briefly.

"The cause is acid rain," she said. "The westerly winds that carry the rain are bringing in the acids. My middle nephew, Euphus here, is ready to prove it."

All eyes turned to Euphus. He bowed to the Mayor and wheeled the cart up to the front table. He handed Rosemary's chart of the pH measurements to the Mayor. The Mayor handed it on to Professor Humwhistel and asked Euphus to proceed.

Euphus began by talking about his school project. He went on to explain about acidity and pH measurements and how the figures were different in each of his columns and why. He also mentioned the rainwater from the Mayor's plaza and invited him to drink some so that he could see for himself how the acid in it made it taste like vinegar. The Mayor thanked him, but declined. Professor Humwhistel congratulated Euphus. The Governor asked the professor for his opinion. Professor Humwhistel stood up.

"The mystery, as Miss Pickerell calls it," he said, smiling, "seems definitely to be limited to the west side of the mountain, since this is where the various problems have occurred. I have verified that on the map that she showed me. It has also been clearly established by Euphus that the acidity is higher on the west side of the mountain. We may therefore assume, I believe, that acidity can be the cause of the problems."

The Council members leaned forward to listen more closely.

"And since the rainwater showed the highest acidity of all," Professor Humwhistel

added, "it may indeed be true that westerly winds are carrying acid rain clouds to Square Toe Mountain. Miss Pickerell has done an excellent job of deduction. It remains only for me to add that rain is most likely to fall from

the clouds in mountainous areas, where they are lifted and cooled. And—"

"We can't stop the rain!" the Mayor cried.

"And," Professor Humwhistel went on, "since our lakes and ponds are not alkaline enough to neutralize the acid rain, our fish are dying. And—"

"We can't stop the rain!" the Mayor called out again.

Professor Humwhistel was so involved in his explanation that he did not even hear the Mayor.

"And," he continued, "acid change is not limited to ponds and lakes. Miss Pickerell mentioned sicknesses and correctly connected them with acids. The acids in the moist air can penetrate the lower lungs and cause serious respiratory damage. The health of the public is unquestionably endangered by acid in the air and in the rain."

The professor sat down. Everyone began to talk at once. The Mayor banged on the table again, this time with both his fists and the gavel.

"We can't stop the rain, Miss Pickerell," he shouted. "Do you know that? Can you give me a solution for that problem?"

The room became hushed. Everybody waited for Miss Pickerell's answer.

"Of course we can't stop the rain, Mr. Mayor," she began. "But . . ."

She paused for a moment to organize her thoughts. Mr. Trilling's voice rang out from the back of the room before she had finished thinking.

"Point of order!" he called to the Mayor. "Point of order!"

"Yes?" the Mayor asked.

"I have been trying to get your attention for the last twenty minutes, your Honor," Mr. Trilling told him, almost screaming out the words. "Miss Pickerell does *not* have the right to the floor. Mrs. Broadribb is next on the agenda. As chairman, you have the responsibility of observing the rules and letting Mrs. Broadribb proceed."

The Mayor nodded his head.

Mrs. Broadribb got up. She talked on and on about the inconveniences of a garbage strike. And not even the Mayor could stop her. She had every right to the floor.

Miss Pickerell lost patience. She walked out of the meeting while Mrs. Broadribb was still talking. Mr. Trilling helped push the cart out and smiled politely. Miss Pickerell did not smile back. She was absolutely boiling with anger.

9

Mapping Out the Bicycle Plan

The Governor and Professor Humwhistel walked out with Miss Pickerell. They seemed to be almost as upset as she was.

"I asked to be excused," the professor explained. "I told the Mayor I had nothing more to say."

"His meeting will go on until daybreak," the Governor mumbled. "And, as always, it will accomplish nothing. Now, on the state level, I handle things differently. I . . ."

"Of course," Miss Pickerell said, barely listening because it was seven o'clock and she was busy giving Nancy Agatha and Pumpkins their medicines. "Of course, we can't stop the rain. But I was about to tell the Mayor that we had to find the place where the *acid* rain was coming from. Then we could put a stop to *that*!"

"Perhaps it was just as well that you didn't tell him," the professor said gently, "since none of us knows the place."

Miss Pickerell sighed. The professor began to help Euphus put the shopping cart into the automobile.

"Aunt Lavinia," Euphus called out. "Can we stop at Mr. Rugby's diner for an eclipse special on the way back? Please?"

Miss Pickerell stared at him. It wasn't so very long ago that he had devoured at least four peanut-butter sandwiches. Euphus knew exactly what she was thinking.

"You didn't give us any dessert," he said, accusingly. "The eclipse special would be the dessert."

"Ah, those eclipse specials!" the Governor exclaimed. "How well I remember the taste of the last one I had in Mr. Rugby's diner! What do you say, Professor? Shall we drown our sorrows in a delicious eclipse special? I can tell my chauffeur to pick up your motorcycle and to meet us at the diner in an hour."

Professor Humwhistel agreed.

Miss Pickerell tried to make up her mind. There was really nothing she could do for her animals at home. A visit to Mr. Rugby's diner might help her to relax. It might even help her to *think*. She nodded her agreement to the eclipse specials.

The Governor and Professor Humwhistel joined her in the front seat of the automobile. The professor kept Pumpkins on his lap. Euphus stayed in the back with his jars. He talked about eclipse specials all the way to the diner.

The neon sign in front of Mr. Rugby's restaurant was all lit up. MOONBURGERS OUR SPECIALTY, it announced. Mr. Rugby liked everybody to know that he had once been on the moon. He told people that he had met Miss Pickerell in the moon cafeteria when he worked there. Miss Pickerell always enjoyed being with Mr. Rugby. He was so jolly and so eager to please.

He was sitting at the cash register near the window when Miss Pickerell drove up to the entrance. He ran out to greet her the moment he noticed.

"Good evening, Miss Pickerell," he called, nearly tripping over the apron that was much too long for him, as he ran. "How nice to see you! And you have brought the Governor! And Professor Humwhistel! And Euphus! I will give you the very best table that I have in my diner. And I will wait on you myself."

He signaled for his helper to take over the

job at the cash register and rapidly led them to the rear of the restaurant. He seated them at the table with the flowered cloth and napkins on it, in the middle of the room. He ran to get the eclipse specials the minute he took the order. He also assured Miss Pickerell that he would keep an eye on her automobile and trailer outside and report to her regularly about the animals.

"They're fine!" he told her the second time he came over to the table to give his report. "As beautiful as ever!"

Miss Pickerell said nothing. Mr. Rugby removed the chef's hat from his round bald head and sat down.

"I can see that you are very agitated, Miss Pickerell," he said. "You have not even touched your eclipse special."

"Euphus can have it," Miss Pickerell replied. "He has already finished his."

Euphus had spooned up all two scoops of Mr. Rugby's homemade cherry ice cream and swallowed every crumb of the sponge cake underneath. He was now leaning over the table and drawing something on the back of a menu.

"Is it the trouble about the mysterious happenings that is worrying you, Miss Pickerell?" Mr. Rugby went on anxiously. "I have been hearing about it over the radio."

"We have tracked the problem down to acid rain," Miss Pickerell informed him. "We now have to find out where that acid rain is coming from."

"We don't have the answer to that question as yet, Mr. Rugby," the professor explained further.

"Personally," the Governor added, "I have no idea how to go about making this search. I also have no hesitation in saying that I don't know *exactly* what we're looking for. How can we when we don't even know who or what is putting the acid into the rain?"

"I know," Euphus said, looking up from his drawing. "I know how we can find where the acid rain comes from. It's easy."

Miss Pickerell and the Governor gasped. Professor Humwhistel gave Euphus a puzzled glance. Mr. Rugby looked very eager.

"And we don't have to know *exactly* what we're looking for," Euphus added, turning to the Governor. "We'll know when we find it."

"May I ask what you have in mind?" the Governor inquired.

"Sure!" Euphus told him. "I wrote it all down on Mr. Rugby's menu."

He passed the menu around the table.

Miss Pickerell, the Governor, and Mr. Rugby inspected it and looked questioningly at each other. Professor Humwhistel seemed to understand. He nodded gravely, as he took his pipe out of his pocket and then put it back again.

"Please go on, Euphus," he said.

"My team and I can start any time," Euphus announced. "We'll look for the acid with our pH meters. We'll begin on the west side of the mountain. We'll know where the acid is coming from when we track down the place with the highest acidity. I told you it was easy."

Miss Pickerell thought the idea was ridiculous.

"You and your friends can hardly walk all over the west side of the mountain and test every bit of soil and water that you see," she said. "That's impossible!"

"But we won't be walking," Euphus told her. "We'll go on our bikes. And we won't be testing the soil and the water. We'll be measuring the air."

"The *air*!" Miss Pickerell, the Governor, and Mr. Rugby exclaimed.

"The air," Euphus repeated. "With helium-filled balloons that have our pH meters attached to them."

"A pH meter with a radio transmitter, I would imagine," Professor Humwhistel commented.

"Battery-powered transmitters that signal the acid measurements back to us on our radios," Euphus said, jumping up and down in his chair with excitement. "We'll turn the meters on and let the balloons go up every twenty minutes. Way up! Up to five hundred feet, maybe. Or even a thousand feet. Then we'll pull them down and follow the scent!!"

"Like Mr. Kettelson's dog does when he smells something he's interested in," Mr. Rugby said, his double chins bouncing up and down as he nodded enthusiastically.

"Mr. Kettelson's dog is a very intelligent animal," Miss Pickerell added.

"But I haven't spoken about the best part," Euphus went on. "It's all figured out on the map. It tells the way we'll be traveling."

Miss Pickerell took another look at the map. It showed how the bicycle riders would fan out from the base of the mountain, each one heading in a different direction. The map also showed the bicycles coming together later and following one another in a single direction. That direction had a big question mark on it.

"That's the direction we'll be going in when one of us reports that he's on the scent," Euphus explained.

"You'll need radios!" Mr. Rugby exclaimed. "And batteries! I'll get them for you. From Mr. Kettelson. I—"

"One moment, Mr. Rugby," Miss Pickerell said. "Euphus has not told us yet who will be organizing the messages about the pH measurements. Someone responsible will need to study those carefully and make the decisions about the direction in which to proceed."

"YOU!" Mr. Rugby shouted. "You are very responsible. You can receive the messages on your farm and send the directions back to Euphus and he can tell his team. I'll get the two-way radios . . ."

Miss Pickerell was not paying any attention to Mr. Rugby. She was watching Professor Humwhistel and the Governor, who were studying the map again.

"I wholly approve of the plan," the Governor said, when he looked up.

"I believe it is an excellent plan," the professor agreed.

"I *don't*," Miss Pickerell said flatly.

"You *don't*?" the Governor and the professor repeated.

"No, I don't," Miss Pickerell told them, emphasizing her statement with a small bang of her unused ice-cream spoon on the table. "I definitely do not approve of children wandering practically all over the state without someone to watch over them."

"It's not *all* over the state," Euphus protested.

"Whether it is or not," Miss Pickerell told him, "you will probably be traveling for hours on end. Isn't that right, Professor?"

"Possibly," the professor replied. "We have no indication how long the search may take and . . ."

"And," Miss Pickerell went on, "I am certain that Euphus's parents would never permit it. I very much doubt that the parents of his teammates would consent to such a venture, either. Not without good adult supervision."

Euphus gave her a very scornful look.

"We don't need anybody to watch over us," he said. "Besides, nobody could. Nobody could follow six bicycles all going off in different directions."

"Not unless that somebody went up in an airplane and watched over them from the sky," Mr. Rugby said, laughing.

Miss Pickerell laughed, too. The Governor and the professor did not even smile. They stared at each other with great seriousness. The Governor spoke first.

"I believe the idea of a plane is a good one," he said. "I also believe that the professor agrees with me."

"Wow!" Euphus shouted, jumping up and down again. "And you'll fly in it, Aunt Lavinia!"

"I can think of no one better," the Governor stated.

"We'll send the messages with the pH measurements to you in the plane," Euphus said, still shouting. "And you can send us back the directions from there. You said you were going to get out on the trail, Aunt Lavinia. You said—"

"On second thought," the Governor went on, trying very hard to speak more loudly than Euphus, "a helicopter might be even better. I can let you have the use of the state helicopter, Miss Pickerell. It is meant for my private use and is called, as you know, *Helicopter Force #1*. And . . ."

He paused and sat up straight in his chair. He looked, Miss Pickerell observed, the way he often looked on television, just before he was about to make a speech.

"This is a most important mission," he said, after he took a breath. "The lives and welfare of the people in our great state await the solution of the acid-rain horror. You, Miss Pickerell, are going out on the trail. For the sake of our beloved state, I will go with you. We will be on the trail together. I will pick you up in my helicopter, Miss Pickerell. At seven o'clock tomorrow morning!"

10

The Search Begins

The standing clock in Miss Pickerell's hallway was striking eight when she walked into her house again. She stopped first in the kitchen to give Pumpkins some clean fresh water and to put some dry food into his bowl for a snack.

"You and Nancy Agatha have had a long day," she told him. "She's resting in the barn now and I suggest you go to sleep, too. I'll just call Mr. Kettelson and ask him to come and take care of you tomorrow, while I'm away. That is, if his chest condition has not gotten any worse."

She called Mr. Kettelson at his hardware store. He stayed open until nine, she knew, to accommodate late shoppers. Mr. Kettelson said he was feeling much the same. But he would certainly come to stay with Pumpkins and Nancy Agatha. He understood very well that Miss Pickerell's mind would be more at ease if he stayed on the farm with them.

"And," he went on to inform her, "I know all about the bicycle trail. Mr. Rugby has already been here to borrow the two-way radio and the transmitters. It has also been announced that the Governor is going to make a speech about the two of you in the helicopter. There will be a special telecast at ten o'clock tonight."

Miss Pickerell heaved a sigh at the very thought of it.

"I'll ask my new assistant to take charge of the store," Mr. Kettelson continued. "And, since I'm sure you won't mind, I'll bring my dog. I'm still giving him the medicine that Dr. Haggerty prescribed."

Miss Pickerell sighed again. She knew all about that.

"I'll leave the medicines for Pumpkins and Nancy Agatha with the directions on the kitchen table," she said. "Dr. Haggerty's schedule is for medication every four hours. I'll attend to the first dose for the day before I leave."

"Do you believe that the medicines are helping?" Mr. Kettelson asked anxiously.

"Not really," Miss Pickerell admitted. "I

didn't see any improvement when I last put some salve around Nancy Agatha's eyes and when I gave Pumpkins his tablets and cough mixture. That was just before I left for Mr. Rugby's diner with Professor Humwhistel, the Governor, and Euphus."

"Mr. Rugby is very confident that Euphus and his friends will track down the cause of our troubles soon," Mr. Kettelson said hopefully.

"Yes, I know," Miss Pickerell commented. "Mr. Rugby feels confident about practically everything."

She thanked Mr. Kettelson and began to get ready for bed. Tomorrow was going to be an even more strenuous day than the one she'd just been through. She drank a glass of warm milk, made sure that both her front and back doors were locked, and went upstairs.

Her bones ached with weariness when she climbed into bed. But her mind was too full of thoughts about what would be happening tomorrow for her to fall asleep.

"I'll have to," she said to Pumpkins, who kept jumping over to face her every time she turned around.

Pumpkins meowed a loud protest. He didn't approve of the tossing and turning.

"I can't help it," Miss Pickerell explained to him, while she rearranged her pillows. "Maybe I ought to count sheep. They say that makes you go to sleep. I think I'd rather count the animals that I know, though."

She was up to Alfred, the friendly bull who lived on Mrs. Pickett's farm, when she fell asleep. The insistent ringing of the telephone woke her up again. It was Euphus.

"We're all ready to go," he announced. "We have maps that I made for everybody and our radios and batteries and balloons and compasses. And we're taking box lunches along. And I forgot to tell you yesterday that we're attaching strong nylon cord to the balloons. Strong and *long* nylon cord. That way, we can haul the balloons down from way up high whenever we want."

"What time is it, Euphus?" Miss Pickerell inquired.

"Don't you know?" Euphus asked. "It's six-thirty."

Miss Pickerell leaped out of bed. She was dressed and downstairs again in ten minutes. She fed Pumpkins and gave him his medicine.

She heard the distant humming of the helicopter when she was racing to the barn to put the salve around Nancy Agatha's eyes and to lead her to the pasture. The helicopter was approaching the lawn by the time she returned. She could see its red, white, and blue colors when she ran back into the house to write the directions down for Mr. Kettelson. He arrived at the kitchen door just as she was placing the salve, the tablets, and the cough mixture on top of the note. Mr. Esticott was right behind him.

"I brought you some coffee and doughnuts and chocolate-chip cookies from our station cafeteria," he said, handing her a paper bag with a container of coffee and a large napkin wrapped around the doughnuts and the cookies. "Miss Lemon, who stopped by the station on her way to work, said she knew you'd be much too excited to think about it yourself and . . ."

"Thank you, Mr. Esticott," Miss Pickerell said, eagerly sipping her coffee and looking around anxiously. "Where's your dog, Mr. Kettelson?"

Mr. Kettelson glanced hesitantly at Mr. Esticott. Mr. Esticott began clearing his throat.

"Mr. Kettelson thought he was coughing too much to be shut up in his carrier," he said finally. "You see, we came up here by bus . . ."

"I was not going to say anything, Miss Pickerell," Mr. Kettelson went on. "I didn't want to worry you. And my assistant is taking good care of him."

But, Miss Pickerell observed, Mr. Kettelson himself was looking very worried. She thrust her coffee aside.

She was pouring the part she had not finished drinking into the sink when she heard more distinct sounds from the helicopter. It was making landing noises now. When she, Mr. Kettelson, and Mr. Esticott rushed to the window, they could see the Governor stepping out onto the lawn. He was dressed in his best dark suit and his hair and mustache were carefully slicked down.

"I have a message for you, Miss Pickerell," he called, as he ran up the kitchen stairs and pushed open the door. "Euphus wants you to know about the nylon cord he is attaching to his balloons."

"He called me about it this morning," Miss Pickerell said.

"He also spoke about it to me and my wife when he telephoned yesterday," the Governor stated. "He has certainly done a very thorough job of preparation. He and his team will be here shortly. We have decided that we'll all be leaving together. Are you ready, Miss Pickerell? Let me help you with your knitting bag and umbrella. And with your doughnuts and chocolate-chip cookies."

Miss Pickerell saw the line of bicycles when she walked out. A bright red balloon flew from each set of handlebars. Euphus, at the head of the line, waved his pH meter at her and pointed to the two-way radios standing next to the lunch boxes in each bicycle basket.

The Governor led the way to the helicopter. Miss Pickerell, together with Mr. Esticott and Mr. Kettelson, followed. Mr. Kettelson held Pumpkins in his arms. Miss Pickerell stopped to kiss Pumpkins before she let the pilot help her get on the helicopter. He strapped her into a seat next to the Governor.

Euphus and his teammates shouted, "We're off!"

Euphus added, "Look, Aunt Lavinia! Look at the television cameras! They're taking pictures of us. And look at Mrs. Pickett and Mrs. Broadribb and Mr. Trilling and Mr. Rugby driving up in his truck!!"

The helicopter rose. It hovered for a moment above the trees. To Miss Pickerell, it sounded much like a noisy gadfly.

"Well," she said, as she checked in her knitting bag for the menu with Euphus's map on it, "the search begins."

The Governor handed Miss Pickerell her umbrella and picked up the shining top hat he had left under his helicopter seat.

"The search begins!" he called out, as he smiled broadly and waved the hat at the eager camera crew below.

11

"Euphus to Miss Pickerell! Euphus to Miss Pickerell!"

The helicopter did not rise very high. Miss Pickerell could clearly make out the bicycles below. They were heading away from the mountain in a westerly direction, some going northwest, some directly west, some southwest. The helicopter circled above them.

"Where's my radio?" Miss Pickerell asked instantly. "The team may be calling in any minute."

"Next to your seat, ma'm," the pilot told her. "On your left side."

Miss Pickerell said she wanted it on her lap. The Governor leaned over to get it for her.

"It's the most convenient place," she explained to him. "I won't have to go reaching anywhere when the calls come in."

A set of earphones came with the radio.

Two tags, one tied to the radio and one to the earphones, had the words STATE PROPERTY on them in very big letters.

"It's an old model," the Governor apologized. "But the state cannot afford replacements. Mr. Kettelson has probably supplied Euphus and his friends with much newer types."

"It doesn't matter," Miss Pickerell said, as she pushed her hat back a little so that she could adjust the earphones. "As long as the earphones keep some of the helicopter noise out. And as long as the two-way system works."

"It works perfectly," the Governor assured her. "You'll know that for yourself when you hear from Euphus."

Miss Pickerell sat back and waited. Nothing sounded in her earphones at first. Then she heard, "Euphus to Miss Pickerell."

"I hear you," Miss Pickerell replied instantly.

"We are currently checking acidity near the mountains," Euphus stated. "We will send you reports as we move along."

"They are checking acidity near the mountains," Miss Pickerell repeated to the Governor. "We have to wait."

"Have a doughnut," the Governor sug-

gested. "Have a doughnut while you're waiting."

Miss Pickerell said that she preferred to
give all her attention to the bicycle riders.

She could see them hoisting their balloons now. They were moving farther and farther away from each other as they fanned out from the base of the mountain and made their separate ways along quiet country roads. The helicopter was making wider and wider circles to keep up with them, while it moved steadily forward. Square Toe City and its outskirts were being left behind. Miss Pickerell was flying over villages and open fields she had never seen before.

"I wish I had remembered to borrow Mrs. Broadribb's bird-watching glasses," she said regretfully, as she peered down through her own glasses. "I could have enjoyed some of this scenery more. And I could certainly have kept a closer watch on those bicycle riders. Heavens! What are they doing now?"

"Bringing their balloons down, I believe," the Governor told her. "They seem to be meeting some interference from the over-hanging trees."

"I prefer for them to be cautious," Miss Pickerell declared.

The Governor agreed. He also suggested a doughnut again. Miss Pickerell said she would rather have a chocolate-chip cookie. A loud rumbling sound hit her eardrums while she was eating the cookie.

"Euphus to Miss Pickerell!" a voice said. "Euphus to Miss Pickerell!"

"Waiting and ready!" Miss Pickerell answered immediately.

"Nothing yet," Euphus reported. "No change in acidity on Bicycles Numbers One, Two, Three, Four, Five, or Six."

"Nothing yet," Miss Pickerell repeated to the Governor.

"I didn't expect anything yet," the Governor told her. "We've gone only a few miles."

"Fifteen," the pilot called from up front. "Fifteen miles west."

"Thank you," Miss Pickerell said.

She looked out at the bicyclists again. They were sending up the balloons now.

"There *must* be increasing acidity here!" she exclaimed. "It has to start somewhere." Look, Governor! The boys have sent their balloons up again!"

But Euphus's report, a number of miles later, was still not very encouraging.

"It's more or less the same, Aunt Lavinia," he said. "No important difference."

And the balloons came down again when the bicycle riders left their country lanes and entered a large town. They had to steer their way through the traffic on the various main streets. Once Miss Pickerell thought she had lost a cyclist when a bakery wagon and two large furniture vans hid him from sight.

"Thank goodness!" she whispered, when she saw him.

She watched closely as the cyclists rode out into open country again. They seemed to be signaling to each other and to be slowing down. She couldn't think why.

"Maybe they've found something," she speculated. "They'll be putting their balloons up again to make sure."

But the balloons did not go up. And the riders were getting off their bicycles and settling themselves in different locations, with their box lunches.

"So soon?" Miss Pickerell gasped.

"Thirty-two miles," the pilot announced.

"They're probably tired," the Governor said.

"I'm sure they are," Miss Pickerell agreed.

But her impatience mounted, as the pilot kept going round and round waiting for the search to resume.

"Ah!" she exclaimed, when she saw Euphus and his friends get up and on their bicycles again.

"They're fanning out still more," the Governor commented.

"Yes," Miss Pickerell murmured.

"And look," the Governor went on. "They have their balloons up again."

"They're down now," Miss Pickerell said twenty minutes later.

"And up once more," the Governor said twenty more minutes later.

Miss Pickerell and the Governor kept watching as the balloons went down and up and down again. Miss Pickerell was getting ready to throw her hands up in despair when she heard Euphus's voice in her earphones again.

"Acid signals for all cyclists getting stronger," he said. "Stronger the farther west we go."

"Keep going!" Miss Pickerell directed. "Keep going west. And watch out you don't fall off your bike."

"What did he say?" the Governor asked. "I couldn't quite hear him. Ask him to talk louder next time."

Miss Pickerell did not need to ask him. Euphus was shrieking the next time he called.

"Euphus to Miss Pickerell," he began again. "Euphus reporting to Miss Pickerell!"

"Yes, yes, Euphus!" she shouted. "Proceed!"

"Acid signals for Bicycles Numbers One, Two, Five, and Six are getting weaker," he called. "Acid signals for Bicycles Numbers Three and Four are stronger."

"Abandon trails Numbers One, Two, Five, and Six," Miss Pickerell ordered. "Follow trails of Bicycles Numbers Three and Four only."

"Right!" Euphus replied. "New directions are being sent to all riders."

"Forevermore!" Miss Pickerell breathed.

"I heard," the Governor nodded. "I heard very distinctly this time. Please tell Euphus to continue to shout when he calls back. The reception on noisy helicopters can be very weak."

But Euphus did not call back. Miss Pickerell kept on looking at her watch. She even pushed the earphones aside for an instant and put her watch up to her ear to make sure the watch was going. The Governor, also checking the time, was beginning to look worried.

"I can't imagine why Euphus has stopped reporting," he said. "I expected him to do so regularly at *this* point."

"Yes," Miss Pickerell murmured.

She was even more worried than the Governor. What if there had been an accident? What if Euphus or one of the other boys had rolled over into a ditch? What . . .?

"Fly a little lower," she called to the pilot. "Fly as close to the cyclists as you can. I want to take a good look at each one of them."

The pilot swooped down in a slow, even circle. Miss Pickerell peered hard through her glasses to scrutinize the team members. They were all there, right on their bikes, pedaling hard. And there was not a ditch in sight. Miss Pickerell relaxed. But only for a moment—

"The radio must have broken down," she told the Governor. "We have lost communication. That's what has happened."

The Governor stared at Miss Pickerell. Miss Pickerell stared at the silent radio. She also told herself not to be so silly.

"Miss Pickerell to Euphus!" she called into the microphone. "Miss Pickerell calling . . ."

Euphus's voice sounded over hers.

"Bad news, Aunt Lavinia!" he cried. "We've gotten off track."

"They've gotten off track," Miss Pickerell repeated to the Governor.

"I heard," the Governor said, his face growing white.

Miss Pickerell returned to the radio.

"Euphus!" she called. "Are you there? Do you hear me?"

"Yes, Aunt Lavinia," Euphus said.

"Then please explain your problem," she told him. "Explain it to me exactly."

"The acid signals on trails Numbers Three and Four just got weaker as we kept going," he told her. "That's all."

Miss Pickerell thought as fast as she could. The first idea that came into her head was that children tended to go to extremes. Rosemary, for example, whenever she tried to cook vegetables, always turned the gas jet on either too high or too low. Euphus might well be doing much the same thing.

Her second idea seemed to her even more likely. Children were very often set in their ways. Euphus was probably so overjoyed with the strong signals on his trails that he just kept going. He didn't . . .

"Euphus!" she shouted to him now. "Listen to me carefully! Go back to where the signals were strongest and start all over again. Proceed more slowly this time. You may have gone too far west. Or you may not have made the change to go even farther west. Along one of these new paths is the direction we are looking for. It is our only possibility! Check every *ten* minutes from now on and report to me!"

The Governor, who had been listening intently to both her and Euphus, was wringing his hands.

"It's hopeless," he said. "What will happen to our great state, Miss Pickerell?"

"We must not give up," Miss Pickerell replied, trying desperately to sound much more confident than she felt. "You told me yourself, Governor, when I was speaking with you on the telephone, that you would not let such events bring you to your knees. You said . . ."

She talked on and on, as much to herself as to the Governor, while she thought of poor Pumpkins and Nancy Agatha and about Mr. Kettelson and his dog and the farmers and their crops and . . .

The radio sounded again, so loudly that it seemed almost to crackle in Miss Pickerell's ears.

"It worked!" Euphus screamed. "We're on track again!! All the signals are pointing in the same direction and the acid is getting higher and higher and higher!!!"

"Forevermore!" Miss Pickerell breathed again.

"But wait a minute, Aunt Lavinia," Euphus continued. "There's something funny going on. Another helicopter is following you. Better take a look, Aunt Lavinia. Better take a look and find out what's happening."

114

12

The Mysterious Stranger

Miss Pickerell did not believe for a minute that they were being followed. After all, she told herself when she looked at the light-gray helicopter behind her, she and the Governor were not the only ones who had the right to airspace.

"My middle nephew, Euphus, has a very vivid imagination, Governor," she said. "I'm sure the pilot in the helicopter behind us is attending to his own business. He simply happens to be flying in the same direction that we are."

"He's much too close for comfort," the Governor replied curtly. "There are strict government regulations about space between flying vehicles. That fellow is up to something."

The Governor's pilot thought so, too.

"He's following every move I make," he said. "He has been doing it for the last five minutes."

"Pick up speed!" the Governor ordered.

His pilot obeyed. He also steered sharply to the left. The helicopter in back did the same. Miss Pickerell could hear its grinding hum close by. She could also see the way the light-gray helicopter took a dive in rapid pursuit when the Governor's pilot made a downward swoop. She put her hands over her eyes to keep herself from seeing any more.

"He's after us, Governor!" the pilot exclaimed. "There's no question about it."

"What—what can he want?" Miss Pickerell stammered from behind her hands.

"*You* have nothing to worry about, Miss Pickerell," the Governor advised her. "It's *me* he's after!"

Miss Pickerell took her hands away from her eyes.

"What—what do you mean?" she whispered.

"This is a *heist*," the Governor, also whispering, replied. "A kidnapping! My State Cabinet has been cautioning me over and over again about that possibility. They have told—"

"Why would anyone want to . . . ?" Miss Pickerell began.

The Governor did not answer.

"Contact the base!" he shouted to the pilot. "Use your radio to contact the base!"

"I'm trying," the pilot replied. "I've been trying."

"Tell them to send reinforcements," the Governor went on. "Tell them to do so immediately. No, I'll come forward to tell them myself."

He unfastened his seat belt and stood up. The cane he leaned on to steady himself creaked under his weight. Miss Pickerell gave him her umbrella.

"No use in that, Governor," the pilot told him. "I haven't been able to make contact yet."

"There are strict government regulations about communications, too," the Governor exploded. "I cannot accept this!"

The gray helicopter was now flying right alongside them. It was so close that Miss Pickerell could easily see the person inside. He was a middle-sized man with red hair that was turning white and a very young face. He wore a neat brown raincoat and had a large briefcase on the seat beside him. Miss Pickerell did not think he looked at all like a kidnapper. But then, she told herself, there was really no telling what kidnappers looked like.

"Maybe I ought to try to radio him and talk to him," the Governor's pilot said. "Maybe it—"

"Never mind that!" Miss Pickerell interrupted. "If you'll just slow up a little and cut down on some of your noise, pilot, I can talk to him personally. Why, he's practically right next door."

The pilot slowed down. Miss Pickerell leaned over as far as she could in her seat.

"Young man!" she called out. "What you are doing is outrageous. It is also, as the Governor has just stated, against all rules and regulations. I *demand* an explanation!"

"Good morning, Miss Pickerell," the man in the gray helicopter called back politely. "I'm here to tell you that it would be most advisable for you and the Governor to make an immediate landing."

"Impossible!" Miss Pickerell said, gasping and beginning to wheeze again.

"Save your breath, Miss Pickerell," the young man told her. "You'll feel better if you do."

Miss Pickerell was about to tell him that his remark bordered on impertinence, but the Governor interrupted.

"Why?" he asked her. "Why does he want us to make an immediate landing? Insist on a *full* explanation!"

"There's no time for that, I'm afraid," the young man replied.

"I most certainly agree with the Governor," Miss Pickerell, drawing in a very deep breath, called out. "I don't know who you are or how you know my name. But if you think for one moment that we are going to interrupt this important journey just because you tell us to, you are very much mistaken. We will never consent to such a step."

"Never!" the Governor repeated. "Never will it be said that the Governor of this great state gave in to the demands of a hijacker."

"A hijacker!" the young man exclaimed in amazement. "What you should be worrying about now, Governor, is the storm that . . ."

"I observe no signs of a storm," the Governor told him sharply. "That is your ploy, your way of trying to get me to land so that you—"

"I see that I will have to stop you," the young man interrupted, "*before* it's too late!"

He moved full speed ahead. Just as quickly, he turned directly to the left.

"He's trying to get ahead of us," the Governor screamed. "He wants to BLOCK OUR WAY!"

The Governor's pilot knew this, too. He flew farther to the left and raced forward. The gray helicopter moved to catch up and came in from the right. The Governor's pilot veered to the left and sped forward. The mysterious stranger roared ahead. He maneuvered a swift curve and moved directly in front of the Governor's helicopter from a sharp right angle.

Miss Pickerell, jolted from side to side in the straps that bound her, felt herself getting dizzier by the minute. Her head was whirling. Her stomach was turning somersaults. And the world seemed to be shrinking to a dark blur before her eyes. When the Governor's pilot jerked to a slowdown to avoid a smashing collision with the helicopter, she was practically sure she was going to faint.

13

The Arrival

The gray helicopter moved back to fly alongside of them again. The man inside leaned over to talk to Miss Pickerell.

"I'm sorry," he said. "I'm sorry I had to do this to you, Miss Pickerell. And to you too, Governor. But you will have to make a landing. I will lead the way."

"Who . . . ?" Miss Pickerell asked, as she lifted her chin from where it had fallen down on her chest and shook her head from side to side to make herself feel more awake. "Who are you?"

"Nathan Lamberson, formerly of the United States Air Force and currently research scientist with the National Environmental Agency, Square Toe City Branch," the young man replied in one quick breath.

He turned his helicopter around and signaled to the Governor's pilot to fly along with him.

"We all heard you, Governor," he said, after the turns were accomplished. "We all heard you announce on radio and television that you, Miss Pickerell, and Euphus were going out into the wilds to save your state from the perils of acid rain. Our agency decided to join you in the effort."

"I am a dues-paying member of that organization," Miss Pickerell stated promptly. "If you continue to interrupt our journey, I will withdraw my membership."

"You didn't describe my speech very well," the Governor added quickly. "Those were *not* my *exact* words. I would prefer for you to quote me more accurately in the future. The idea, of course, is correct. We are on an urgent mission trying to save—"

Peals of thunder interrupted the Governor's statement.

"Right now," Mr. Lamberson remarked, "it seems more urgent to save ourselves from the perils of the weather."

"Pooh!" Miss Pickerell said. "A little thunder never hurt anyone."

"But my agency has communicated the latest weather report to me," Mr. Lamberson

123

told her. "My chief has *advised* me to bring you to safety."

"I'm not going to tell on you to your chief, if that's what is bothering you," Miss Pickerell retorted. "I'm perfectly capable of holding my tongue when necessary."

"And I wish to go on record as saying," the Governor stated, "that the Square Toe Branch of the National Environmental Agency does not run this state. Your agency is not government-sponsored and it has no authority to—"

"Governor!" Mr. Lamberson burst out. "You are flying smack INTO what may well turn into a tornado. The revised weather forecast has predicted a storm with all the violence of a RAGING SEA!"

The Governor looked nervously at Miss Pickerell.

"What do you . . . ?" he began.

She didn't answer him.

"Euphus!" she exclaimed. "I haven't heard from him lately. And I haven't been . . ."

"I see him," Mr. Lamberson told her. "I see the whole team."

Miss Pickerell leaned back in her seat. But she sat up straight again when she heard the Governor's pilot talking.

"The base has just reported news of the

impending storm," he was saying. "One of the worst we've ever had. I'm heading for a landing."

Euphus's voice came in on the radio before anyone had a chance to comment.

"Euphus to Miss Pickerell," he said. "Euphus to Miss Pickerell."

"Never mind that nonsense," Miss Pickerell told him. "Is it raining down where you are?"

"Of course not," Euphus said. "You can see that for yourself, Aunt Lavinia."

"Yes," Miss Pickerell agreed quickly.

"We're on Route 101 now," Euphus went on. "The mileage gauge on my bike says we've traveled a hundred twenty miles. And the acidity is the highest we've had yet. And we can smell smoke. It's drifting westward and when the wind blows, Aunt Lavinia, the smoke has that vinegary taste like the one in my rain jars. I know because the wind blew some into my mouth and—"

"How long do you think it will be before you track down this smoke?" Miss Pickerell broke in quickly.

"Oh, five minutes!" Euphus told her. "Ten, maybe."

She jumped up in her seat to speak to the Governor's pilot.

"Call your base," she commanded. "Find out exactly when they expect this tornado, or whatever it is, to start in earnest."

"Nothing can be seen from up here!" the Governor shouted into the radio.

Miss Pickerell paid no attention.

"Yes, ma'm," the pilot replied.

"If it is under ten minutes, turn the helicopter around and go in the direction that Euphus and his team are taking."

In approximately one minute the Governor's pilot was maneuvering the helicopter around to its original position.

"You can't do that!" Mr. Lamberson shouted.

"And who is telling me not to?" Miss Pickerell shouted back. "You who have never seen how my friend Mr. Kettelson looked when he had to inform me that his dog was very sick? You, who—"

"Turn that helicopter back before I force you to do it!" Mr. Lamberson called to the Governor's pilot.

The pilot began making a reverse turn.

"No!" Miss Pickerell screamed. "Don't listen to him! He has probably never even heard of crops failing and birds dying and flowers shriveling and—"

126

"Not true!" Mr. Lamberson called out. "I care a lot about all those things. And I grow nasturtiums and lettuce in my own yard."

"We can't keep going back and forth this way forever, Mr. Lamberson," Miss Pickerell replied, trying hard to ignore the wheezing that was acting up again, and practically seething with exasperation. "The time is short. It's not raining yet and—"

Euphus's voice broke in again.

"We're moving straight ahead," he said. "The smoke is the worst there. We don't know yet where it's coming from, but we sure know the direction to take."

"The smoke is straight ahead," she repeated to Mr. Lamberson. "Euphus doesn't know yet where it's coming from, but—"

She stopped abruptly when she saw the chimneys. They were big and tall and thick black smoke was belching out of them. Mr. Lamberson saw them, too.

"Smokestacks!" he shouted.

Miss Pickerell opened her mouth and closed it again. She stared at Mr. Lamberson.

"The acid chemicals are coming out of those smokestacks," he said. "Tell your middle nephew to keep going, Miss Pickerell. By all means, to keep going."

"Miss Pickerell to Euphus!" Miss Pickerell called. "Miss Pickerell to Euphus! Are you there? Can you see the tall chimneys ahead? Can you see the smoke belching out of those smokestacks? Keep right on until you reach them, Euphus. We'll meet you at those smokestacks."

"Full speed ahead!" the Governor advised his pilot.

"Full speed ahead!" Mr. Lamberson echoed.

They landed in the midst of the fiercest burst of thunder Miss Pickerell had ever heard. Euphus and his friends were just arriving. Balloons held up in front of them like flags, they rode around and around to encircle the building with the smokestacks.

14

The Confrontation

The building, Miss Pickerell observed when she set foot on the patch of dry grass in front of it, resembled an unpainted old warehouse. It sat stiffly on top of a hill and overlooked a row of small shops across the street. Beyond that, as the hill descended, there seemed to be a park.

Miss Pickerell also saw that the building stretched over an entire city block and that *ten* absolutely enormous smokestacks rose from its sixth-story roof. She rubbed her eyes when she examined them and counted the number over three times to make certain she was not making a mistake. When she came closer to the building, she read the metal sign that was nailed above the entrance door. The sign said: THOMAS A. FLINTSTONE ELECTRIC POWER-GENERATING PLANT. Mr. Lamberson, standing beside her and also reading the sign, commented that the plant was undoubtedly powered by fossil fuels.

"That would account for the acid in the chimneys," he said. "You see, the fossil fuels, such as petroleum, coal, or natural gas, can . . ."

Miss Pickerell was only half listening. She was wondering what had happened to Euphus and his friends. She stopped worrying when she saw them make a dash for the candy store across the street.

"I have a general idea of what you mean, Mr. Lamberson," she said, turning her attention back to him. "And I certainly intend to discuss it with Mr. Thomas A. Flintstone."

"I will have something to say, as well," the Governor, who had been writing the name of the plant down in his pocket address book, added.

Mr. Lamberson smiled.

"I imagine we all will," he said. "I plan to—why, there's Euphus!"

Euphus, waving his red balloon frantically, was racing across the street and shouting for them to wait for him.

"That's a pretty good candy store," he said, panting, when he reached them. "But I wanted to—"

"My heartiest congratulations!" the Governor boomed out, interrupting. "You and your team have performed a heroic service. I will personally recommend citations for your team members and the awarding of a bronze medal to you."

Euphus blushed faintly. Miss Pickerell, who had been about to kiss him, decided against the idea. It would only embarrass him. She was just getting ready to tell him, however, that she thought he deserved the medal, when the storm broke out. The Governor was the first to rush into the plant doorway. Miss Pickerell, Mr. Lamberson, and Euphus quickly followed.

The rain poured from the sky in heavy, slanting sheets. They beat like stones against the factory walls. Mr. Lamberson, looking at Miss Pickerell, had a very satisfied smile on his face.

But the rain stopped almost as suddenly as it had started. Mr. Lamberson's smile changed to an expression of utter surprise.

"Those weather forecasters!" Miss Pickerell said, scornfully. "They're all alarmists. They *like* to make things sound worse."

"They like to be *cautious*," Mr. Lamberson corrected her.

He walked rapidly into the lobby and toward the wall board that listed the names and the room numbers. The information about Mr. Thomas A. Flintstone was near the top of the list. His office was one flight up, on the second floor. There was an escalator nearby.

Miss Pickerell disliked escalators almost as much as express elevators. She particularly disliked the very long escalators with the big spaces between the treads. Going down sometimes put her into a panic. But going up was not so bad. She transferred her knitting bag and umbrella to her left hand, grasped the banister with her right one, and got on. The Governor and Mr. Lamberson helped her to get off.

Mr. Flintstone's office was about halfway down the second-floor corridor, not very far away from a row of three public-telephone booths. Miss Pickerell knocked on his door immediately.

"Come in," a gruff voice answered.

Mr. Thomas A. Flintstone looked even more gruff than he sounded. He was a heavyset man, with a weather-beaten face and piercing blue eyes that inspected Miss Pickerell, the Governor, Mr. Lamberson, and Euphus with instant suspicion.

"Well?" he asked.

"We have come about your chimneys,"
Miss Pickerell said. "I am Miss Pickerell.
And this is—"

Mr. Flintstone cut short the introductions.

"What about my chimneys?" he wanted to know.

"They are discharging sulfuric and nitro-

gen oxides from the fossil fuels you are using," Mr. Lamberson said heatedly.

Mr. Flintstone shrugged his shoulders.

"I use coal and oil," he said. "It cuts down on oil bills. If this oil shortage is ever over, I may—"

"We don't know when it will be over," Mr. Lamberson interrupted. "And in the meantime, you are creating serious damage. The oxides released from your chimneys change chemically as they travel through the atmosphere and become acids. The acids can be carried by winds for hundreds, sometimes thousands of miles. When they are washed out of the air by the rain, they create damage wherever they go."

"I don't know what you're talking about," Mr. Flintstone replied bluntly.

"I will try to be more specific," Mr. Lamberson said. "I will begin with the soil. When acid rain falls on the earth, vegetation is assaulted from both above and below. The leaves are attacked from above. The roots in the soil below are starved and poisoned. They—"

"Excuse me," the Governor broke in. "I would also like to say a few words about acid rain. I am the Governor of my great state and I can tell you officially that our crops have been severely damaged, our lakes and rivers ruined, and our trout and salmon all killed."

Mr. Lamberson nodded and opened his briefcase.

"I made sure to bring this with me from the helicopter," he said, taking out a magazine and opening it up quickly. "It is the latest issue put out by the National Environmental Agency. This article on page twenty-two notes even more exactly than I did what your smokestacks are doing. It explains that coal and oil-fired power plants, as they burn their fuel, release sulfur dioxide and various nitrogen oxides, which combine with oxygen. This results in the formation of sulfuric acid from the sulfur dioxide and the formation of nitric acid from the nitrogen oxides. It is really not too difficult to understand that, Mr. Flintstone."

"I understood it," Euphus volunteered.

Mr. Flintstone ignored Euphus.

"I have already been informed about that article," he said, frowning. "But you are mistaken about what is happening here. My smokestacks are nearly five hundred feet tall. I had them built that way purposely. They clear the air."

"Clear the air!" Mr. Lamberson snorted.

"They're doing no such thing. They are doing exactly the *opposite*. They are kicking the oxides higher, right out into the prevailing westerly winds! They are—"

"My nephew here can prove it," Miss Pickerell cut in. "He can show you the pH readings. And Mr. Lamberson hasn't even mentioned the respiratory and other sicknesses that are the result of those chemicals coming out of your tall chimneys."

"What do you want me to do?" Mr. Flintstone barked at Mr. Lamberson. "Change back to smaller chimneys?"

"Not at all," Mr. Lamberson replied quickly. "They would *not* help at all. Smaller chimneys would not clear the air even locally. My agency recommends scrubbers."

"To clean the smoke coming out of the chimneys," Miss Pickerell said, approvingly. "I'm sure that's right."

"For tall chimneys," Mr. Lamberson went on, "we recommend *superscrubbers*. They can remove the oxides from your chimneys."

"And they can also force me into bankruptcy," Mr. Flintstone stormed. "Yes, I know I can install superscrubbers. To the tune of $100,000 I can. I won't have any profits left over to remain in business."

"Mr. Flintstone—" Mr. Lamberson began.

"No," Mr. Flintstone said. "I have listened to you long enough. Now, you listen to me. I am a self-made man. I have built this business up from scratch. And I am a good citizen, as well as a careful businessman. I have heard the President tell us to save oil and I have cut down on my own use of it. I can do no more. I simply do not have $100,000 to spend on superscrubbers."

"Ask the Governor for it!" Euphus shouted. "Get the money from the Governor!"

Miss Pickerell gave the Governor an eager glance immediately. The Governor calmly looked back at her.

"I am responsible only for my own jurisdiction," he said. "As we began to descend in the helicopter, I observed that we had crossed the state line."

"Then ask the Governor of *this* state," Euphus went on, still shouting. "Get the money from *him.*"

Mr. Flintstone laughed bitterly.

"Nothing doing in that direction," he said. "Our governor is no more able to provide $100,000 for antipollution than I am. He's thinking of raising taxes so that he can keep on paying teachers their salaries."

Miss Pickerell looked around her. No one

had anything to say. The Governor was shaking his head. Mr. Lamberson was staring straight ahead of him. Even Euphus was quiet.

"So, that's *that*," she said to herself glumly.

15

"Call the President, Miss Pickerell"

Miss Pickerell was the first one to leave Mr. Flintstone's office. The Governor and Euphus walked out after her. Mr. Lamberson lagged a little behind. He looked very grim.

"I didn't realize that this state was not in your jurisdiction," Miss Pickerell said to the Governor, as they walked in the direction of the DOWN escalator and she gave a horrified glance at its length.

"This state is definitely *not* in my jurisdiction," the Governor stated. "I have already told you, Miss Pickerell, a Governor has jurisdiction over his *own* state and no more."

"Only the President has jurisdiction over all the states," Euphus chimed in.

Miss Pickerell stopped short in her tracks.

"Did you say, Euphus, that the President has jurisdiction over *all* the states?" she asked.

"Of course," Euphus replied. "Didn't you know that?"

"Yes, yes, I knew," Miss Pickerell told him. "I just didn't happen to think of it."

Euphus laughed. Miss Pickerell did not. She felt more like groaning. Euphus had given her an idea. But it was a terrifying idea. Her knees trembled when she considered what it involved.

"I . . . I must not be such a coward," she said, talking out loud to herself. "Or so silly, either. There is really nothing to be afraid of."

The Governor looked at her hesitantly.

"Were you about to say that you needed some help going down the escalator?" he asked.

"No," Miss Pickerell replied, though she gratefully held onto his hand while the two of them stepped onto the first tread. "No, I was about to say that I have just made up my mind. I am going to call up the President."

The Governor made strange, choking sounds in his throat.

Euphus, standing behind the Governor, called out, "Wow!"

The Governor told him to be quiet.

"You can't bother the President with your

problems, Miss Pickerell," he went on, shouting almost as loudly as Euphus.

Miss Pickerell tried hard to stay calm.

"I wouldn't *dream* of bothering the President with my *own* problems," she said icily. "But acid rain is *not* my own problem. It affects the . . ."

She paused to concentrate on getting off the escalator. Mr. Lamberson, standing next to Euphus, bent over to rescue her umbrella, which dragged behind when she stepped away from the last tread. He also whispered, "Call the President, Miss Pickerell! *Do* call the President!"

Miss Pickerell thanked Mr. Lamberson.

"Mr. Flintstone and I have both listened to the President," she went on, talking to the Governor again. "I have definitely heard him make speeches about amendments to the Clean Air Act. I don't remember precisely which amendments he had in mind, but . . ."

"I can tell you," Mr. Lamberson offered.

"Not now," Miss Pickerell said. "I need to sort out my thoughts."

She walked over to the lobby newsstand and sat down on the corner of a bench piled up with empty boxes. She said she wanted nobody to disturb her for a while. Mr. Lamberson used the time to glance at the latest newspaper headlines. Euphus inspected the candy bars stacked up behind the newspapers. The Governor stared impatiently at his watch.

"I am ready *now*," Miss Pickerell told him, when she got up and began walking briskly toward the UP escalator. The Governor, Euphus, and Mr. Lamberson followed her.

"Where are you going?" the Governor asked anxiously.

"To the telephone booths," Miss Pickerell told him. "To the public-telephone booths that I saw upstairs. I have decided on what I am going to say to the President."

"Please . . . please don't mention my name!" the Governor pleaded.

Miss Pickerell assured him that she had no such intention.

"I am going to tell the President three things," she said. "The first is that the health and welfare of one great state and of another neighboring state, both under his jurisdiction, are in grave danger."

The Governor looked very relieved. He nodded his approval several times.

"The second," Miss Pickerell continued, "is that more of his amendments should be about the compulsory use of superscrubbers.

And the third is about the money for Mr. Flintstone's chimneys. I will tell him so immediately."

The Governor, Euphus, and Mr. Lamberson followed her onto the escalator. This time Miss Pickerell got on without even thinking of being frightened. But her knees shook so violently when she neared the top that she wondered about changing her mind.

"I don't even know how to talk to the President," she said, half to herself, as she walked toward the telephone booths.

"He's easy to talk to," Mr. Lamberson, who heard her, commented. "My chief talks to him all the time."

"I'll talk to him," Euphus offered.

Miss Pickerell paused to think a little more.

"Of course, it's possible," she said, hopefully, "that I may not be *able* to talk to him. You've no idea, Mr. Lamberson, the trouble I had getting hold of the Mayor in his office yesterday. At one point, I was transferred to Bridges and Tunnels."

"That wouldn't happen in *my* office," the Governor said quickly.

"You won't have that difficulty if you use the number my chief has," Mr. Lamberson said. "It connects you with one of the President's secretaries."

Miss Pickerell began walking again. She came to another halt in front of the telephone booths. But she hesitated for only a second.

"My recommendations are very *practical*," she said. "I see no reason at all why I shouldn't tell them to the President!"

"Good for you!" Mr. Lamberson shouted. "I'll dial the number for you."

Miss Pickerell took an exceptionally deep breath when he handed her the phone. She also straightened her hat.

"This is Miss Pickerell of Square Toe Farm," she said resolutely. "I wish to talk to the President of the United States."

The secretary, who turned out to be a man, asked her to repeat and to spell out her name. The connection, after she did so, took almost no time.

"Good afternoon, Miss Pickerell," the President's voice said. "What a pleasure this is! You see, I know all about you. I know about your trips to Mars and the moon and about the speech you made in the British Parliament. I even know about the tea you had with the Queen in Buckingham Palace."

Miss Pickerell's knees stopped trembling. She poured out her heart to the President. She spoke about Pumpkins and Nancy Agatha and all the other problems that had come from the acid-rain crisis. She told him about Mr. Flintstone's chimneys and the money question and about the jurisdiction difficulty and about her middle nephew, Euphus, and his water samples. And about how Euphus, who was at the head of the bicycle trail to the chimneys, had said that all fifty states were under the President's jurisdiction.

"I guess they are," the President laughed. "We'll see what we can do."

"When, Mr. President?" Miss Pickerell asked anxiously.

"You just wait at that electric-generating plant, Miss Pickerell," the President told her. "It may take a couple of hours. But, never fear, you'll hear from me!"

16

The Solution

Euphus, Mr. Lamberson, and the Governor were pressing so hard against the closed door of the telephone booth that Miss Pickerell could hardly make her way out.

"What? What? What? What?" they all asked.

"I forgot . . . I forgot to tell him about the amendments," Miss Pickerell moaned, as she stepped forward.

"But what did he say?" the Governor pleaded. "What did *he* say, Miss Pickerell?"

"That he would see what he could do," Miss Pickerell replied. "In a couple of hours. He told me to wait here."

The Governor nearly pushed her aside in his haste to get into the booth.

"Operator!" he screamed. "Get me the *Square Toe Gazette*, Main Street, Square Toe

City! No, connect me with Television Channel 1313 first! Yes, this will be a collect call. All the calls I will be making are to be collect. This is Governor . . ."

Miss Pickerell shuddered. She knew exactly what was going to happen next. There would be headlines everywhere. The newspaper and television and radio writers would be swarming in with their cameras and their notebooks and reporting all kinds of stories *before* there was even anything to report.

"I'm going out for a walk," she said to Euphus and Mr. Lamberson, who were inside the other two telephone booths.

"Don't go too far away," Mr. Lamberson called out. "I'm waiting for somebody to get on the line or I'd go with you."

Miss Pickerell said that she would definitely be back before the President's couple of hours were up.

"I'll go find another telephone booth," she told herself, "so I can call up Mr. Kettelson."

She met Mr. Flintstone as she walked toward the escalator. He helped her get on and off.

"Where are you going, Miss Pickerell?" he asked.

"I'm not sure," she replied.

Mr. Flintstone gave her a puzzled glance. He was going out for some lunch, he told her.

Miss Pickerell did not feel the least bit hungry. It was almost two o'clock and she had had only Mr. Esticott's coffee for breakfast and some chocolate-chip cookies on the helicopter. But she was much too tired to think about food. She just wanted to call her farm and to walk a little and then to sit down in some quiet place for a while.

She crossed the street to look for a shop with a telephone. There was one in the candy store which, on closer inspection, turned out to be an ice-cream parlor. Euphus's friends were still there. They were sitting around a table filled with desserts that were even fancier than Mr. Rugby's most elaborate eclipse special. They were also listening to rock music on a juke box, which they had turned on to a deafening pitch. Miss Pickerell quickly decided not to make her telephone call there.

The barber shop next door had a red-and-white striped pole outside and a shoeshine stand inside. But there was no telephone.

The drugstore, a few doors away, was quiet and it had a telephone. It also had a brass and marble soda fountain. Mr. Flintstone was sitting there, eating a sandwich.

"They have very good tuna fish here, Miss Pickerell," he said. "I suggest that you try it."

The sandwich looked tempting, Miss Pickerell agreed. She thought she might order one when she finished talking with Mr. Kettelson.

Mr. Kettelson answered her call immediately. He was very excited. He had heard from Euphus's mother only a few minutes ago. Euphus had just called her collect to say that Miss Pickerell had spoken to the President in his Oval Office and that . . .

"I don't know anything about an Oval Office," Miss Pickerell said irritably. "Please tell me about the animals, Mr. Kettelson."

Mr. Kettelson replied that he was about to put some more salve around Nancy Agatha's eyes and to give Pumpkins his medication. His own dog was taking the same tablets and cough mixture.

"My assistant may take him up to the farm later in Mr. Rugby's truck," he said happily.

Mr. Flintstone was no longer at the soda counter when Miss Pickerell sat down for her sandwich. It didn't taste quite as good as it had looked. And the tea she ordered wasn't nearly as hot or as strong as she liked.

"We charge extra for another tea bag," the

man behind the counter told her. "But I can give you some more hot water."

Miss Pickerell settled for the hot water.

It was only three o'clock when she left the drugstore. Miss Pickerell wandered in the direction of the park.

She changed her mind when she saw the concrete playground, which she had not noticed from the top of the hill. There wasn't a blade of grass or a bit of soft soil anywhere. Children on the sliding boards were landing on hard concrete blocks.

"I suppose children will play anywhere," she murmured sadly. "But oh, how I wish the world could be a little different so that they didn't have to."

She turned to walk back to the drugstore. She didn't believe the man behind the counter would mind if she sat there for a while. She'd think of something to order.

"Another cup of tea," she said, when she sat down. "With *two* tea bags this time."

No one else was sitting at the counter. Miss Pickerell spread the crossword puzzle she took out of her knitting bag alongside her teacup. She had been working on the puzzle since Sunday, but she still wasn't able to figure out some of the words. The ones in the right-hand corner were a complete mystery to her. How could *anyone* be expected to know a five-letter word for "ragged crest"?

"Well, I'll just keep trying," she told herself. "It will help to pass the time."

But she couldn't really concentrate. And when she put the puzzle back into her knitting bag and took out the red scarf she was crocheting for her oldest niece, Rosemary, she decided against trying to work on that, too.

"I'd better get back," she told herself. "I haven't stayed out *quite* as long as I expected, but I can't seem to think of anything to do."

It was when she was crossing the street in front of the Thomas A. Flintstone Electric Power-Generating plant that she saw the Governor running out of the building. He was racing toward the patch where his *Helicopter Force #1* was parked and looking up at the sky. Another helicopter was up there, slowing down for a landing.

A crowd gathered around it the instant it touched ground. Euphus was there and the Governor and Mr. Lamberson and Mr. Flintstone and the people from his factory and the dozens of reporters and cameras that Miss Pickerell had expected. Mr. Lamberson looked up and down, trying to find her. He ran to lead her to the helicopter. A woman in a neatly pressed blue suit stepped out of the helicopter and walked up to her immediately.

"Good afternoon, Miss Pickerell," she said, shaking her hand. "I'm your State Senator. The President telephoned me at my office in the State Capitol to ask me to deliver his report to you personally. He thought it would be the fastest way. I came at once."

"Oh!" Miss Pickerell gasped, as she held on tight to the handle of her umbrella to steady her nerves.

The Senator looked at both the knitting bag and the umbrella and smiled.

"I'd have recognized you anywhere, Miss Pickerell," she said. "But to get back to the report. Briefly, it is this: The President called an emergency conference about the dangers of acid rain and the need to eliminate it. Legislation will be introduced to mandate super-scrubbers for all coal- and oil-burning plants and to provide loans for this purpose. The President has promised to see this legislation through Congress and to sign the bill. He extends his deepest appreciation to you, Miss Pickerell. And so do I. You have performed heroically in the interests of our country."

"It was Euphus," Miss Pickerell stammered. "Euphus and his team. And the Governor. And Mr. Lamberson . . ."

155

"The President has repeated the conversation you had with him about the people who helped," the Senator said. "I congratulate them, too. I congratulate Euphus, especially. I understand from the President that it was all his idea."

Euphus grinned.

"And I most certainly congratulate my very good friend, the Governor, who never stops working for the benefit of our great state," the Senator went on. "And naturally, Mr. Lamberson and his diligent and knowledgeable Environmental Agency."

The Governor bowed. Mr. Lamberson nodded his head. Euphus ran off to get his team. Flashbulbs popped. Reporters rushed everywhere, asking questions and making notes on their pads. Miss Pickerell barely answered the questions they asked her. She was too busy listening to the drone of still another helicopter overhead. It was the blue-and-white Square Toe City Police helicopter and it was full of passengers. Mr. Lamberson helped her to squeeze through the crowd so that she could get to it.

Mr. Rugby, screaming, "The President made a speech and we heard everything," was the first one to get off. The Mayor, Assistant Sheriff Swiftlee, Professor Humwhis-

tel, Mr. Esticott, Mrs. Broadribb, and Mr.
Trilling followed. Rosemary, holding Pumpkins in one hand and a shiny hat box in the
other, came last.

"I couldn't bring the cow," she called out
to Miss Pickerell. "Nancy Agatha is too big
for a helicopter. But I brought you your new
hat for when they take all those pictures of

157

you. And Miss Lemon sent a matching straw collar she got in the five-and-dime store for Pumpkins. Wait, let me help you put the hat on."

The reporters and television crews rushed toward Miss Pickerell when she picked Pumpkins up. The Governor and Euphus ran to stand alongside of her. Euphus's team crowded in behind them. Mr. Lamberson stood next to the boys.

"Hurray for Miss Pickerell," the Mayor screamed.

"Speech! Speech!" Mr. Esticott shouted.

"Speech! Speech!" the crowd shouted after him.

Miss Pickerell hugged Pumpkins and held him close to her.

"Everybody here has already talked about everything," she said. "All I can think of is that Pumpkins is going to get better soon. He and so many others . . ."

The crowd roared its applause.

About the Authors

ELLEN MACGREGOR created the character of Miss Pickerell in the early 1950s. With a little help from Miss MacGregor, Lavinia Pickerell had four remarkable adventures. Then, in 1954, Ellen MacGregor died. And it was not until 1964, after a long, long search, that Miss P. finally found Dora Pantell.

DORA PANTELL says that she has been writing something at some time practically since she was born. Among the "somethings" are scripts for radio and television, magazine stories, newspaper articles, books for all ages, and, of course, the Miss Pickerell adventures, which, she insists, she enjoys best of all. As good places for writing, she suggests airplanes, dentists' waiting rooms, and a semidark theater when the play gets dull. Ms. Pantell spends a good deal of the rest of her time reading nonviolent detective stories, listening to classical music on Stations WNCN, and WQXR and watching the television shows on Channel 13 in New York City. But mostly she is busy keeping the peace among her three cats, Haiku Darling, Eliza Doolittle, and the newest addition, the incorrigible Cluny Brown.

159

About the Artist

CHARLES GEER has been illustrating for as long as he can remember and has more books to his credit than he can count. He lives in a rambling old house on the Chesapeake, on Maryland's Eastern Shore. When he is not bent over the drawing board or the typewriter—Mr. Geer has written as well as illustrated two middle-group books—he is at work on the twenty-two-foot sailboat he built himself, or taking long backpack hikes, or sailing.